OPUS ADVENTURE

A STORY OF SURVIVAL & PREPAREDNESS

BOYD CRAVEN

To be notified of new releases, please sign up for my mailing list at:
http://eepurl.com/bghQb1

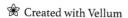 Created with Vellum

RICK

I had slowed my frenetic pace of writing to a more manageable level. I was listening, but I knew if the tyrant awoke, Ophelia would let me know. Her, or her son, Sarge. I smiled, remembering the feigned outrage when we'd named our newest family member after Bud. He pretended to hate it, but the old man had smiled when he'd met the pup.

"Dadadadadadada," the monitor erupted in noise, and I heard a low bark from the other room and the padding of feet as both dogs scrambled to charge into the office.

Ophelia launched herself onto my old futon, a relic from the days when I'd lived with Al in the small two-bedroom apartment. She made a happy whining sound before sticking her nose on my neck. Sarge ran up and grabbed the cuff of my shirt and backed up gently.

"Ok, ok, I can hear—"

"Dayeeeee!" I heard from both the monitor and the bedroom.

I walked into the bedroom where we'd set up the crib. I'd offered to dismantle my office and take over space either in the mini-storage's office or out in the barn that Tina still ran her eBay business from. Owen was standing up, rubbing his eyes, his hair a mass of blond curls that were all sticking straight up.

"Hey, little man, have a good nap?"

Behind me Sarge barked once excitedly, and Owen looked over at him and started giggling.

"More eat?"

"You hungry or thirsty?" I asked him.

"Bubba!" Owen said, then buried his head into my neck.

"I can do that, but first, let's get you a dry deedee on."

He'd been learning his words at an alarming rate. I would like to be proud, but I was finding myself censoring my words and avoiding innuendo around him. For example, deedee meant he had a wet or stinky diaper. I carried him over to the changing table and got out the instruments that prevented weapons of mass destruction being flung or sprayed about the room.

Ophelia jumped on the bed to watch, but Sarge remained at my side, sitting on his haunches. I had his little human, and he knew it. I marveled at how fast the nearly two-year-old son of mine had picked up language. I'd nearly fallen off the chair in our small living room when he'd said, 'delicious eat'. I wasn't even sure that's what he really meant, but he'd grabbed me by the thumb and said, 'pull' and led me to the kitchen. He had gotten frustrated, so I'd picked him up and he'd pointed at the freezer. I'd opened it, and he'd pointed to the Haagen Dazs and repeated 'delicious eat,' much to Tina's amusement.

So of course, I'd done what every new, first-time dad did: I'd made myself ready for a battle, and we'd eaten ice cream for dinner. I think Tina had only taken about four-teen hours of video.

"Oh hey," Tina said, walking into the bedroom just as I was getting the fresh diaper fastened. "I didn't hear him cry, sorry."

"I stole the monitor from you. Besides, the K9 alarms would have gotten me first. I'm closer."

"I can move the Pack-n-Play into the office if you have more work to do."

"Sure thing," I said, snapping his onesie back up. "Need a hand?"

Ophelia took off like a shot and Sarge followed, their nails scratching across the floor.

"In a sec, sounds like we have a customer." She leaned in and kissed me, then hurried after the four-footed furry companions.

"You, sir, are the luckiest baby man alive," I told him, pulling the bedroom door closed, then my office door too, before putting him on the floor.

He wobbled, then took off like a shot, yelling psychobabble that only babies could understand. I grinned and headed into the living room. The Pack-n-Play was a simple affair: take out the bottom of it, pull a red rope coming out of the middle, then collapse the sides with built-in buttons. I did all of that while listening to Owen laugh in the office, just past the kitchen. I carried it with me and saw that Tina had left the door open between the office and the living area of the building. We'd been doing that more and more.

Both of us still had our own respective nightmares and, although we were getting over them, I could see how much we had moved on for the better. Both dogs saw me head for the door and took off ahead of me. Ophelia and Sarge hit the jamb at the same time, sticking and letting out playful barks. By the time I got there, both had tumbled into the other room. Owen was laughing and clapping his pudgy baby hands together shouting "All right" like he'd learned when I'd taught him how to high five.

Opus was sitting next to Tina, alert but relaxed, and watching over the developing craziness like an old grizzled soldier watching the greenhorns work off nervous energy before being deployed. He saw me and chuffed before walking over.

"Hey, buddy, you keeping an eye on things?" I asked him.

"You mean—"

Opus turned to Tina and sneezed then put his head under my outstretched hand. I rubbed his head, scratching behind his ears. "Of course, you're watching everything. Want to go outside and play with Ophelia and Sarge a minute?" I asked.

He chuffed then barked once, his butt wiggling as his tail started to wag. I set the baby gear down and put it together under Owen and Tina's watchful gaze then picked the little man up.

"No, Dayee, owwwwwwwn. Owee wan owwwwwwwwwwn."

"Assert your male dominance," Tina said, grinning.

I put him in the Pack-n-Play and got a scrunched up face in response, Owen quickly turning an alarming shade of red. I turned before I could see the tears start falling and came out around the counter. Sarge and Ophelia were spinning circles in front of me in excitement. Opus was a little more reserved, but when I opened the door, he ran out after them, barking happily.

"We don't have anybody back there right now do we?" I asked, suddenly realizing three dogs over a hundred pounds each might scare the bejeebers out of somebody.

"Nope, it's been a quiet morning. I had somebody come in wanting to rent a space, but she forgot her ID so she went back to get it."

"Ok good," I said.

I felt Tina wrap her arms around my sides and back and I put an arm around her, hugging her tightly, my heart feeling so full. More so than I could ever remember in my lifetime.

"Dayeeeee, owwwwwwww!" Owen demanded from behind me.

"If you want to get more words in, I've got this," Tina told me. "You know, you don't have to steal the monitor from me when you're working. I've done, like, three crosswords and beat three levels of Candy Crush already."

I grinned and kissed the top of her head. "Maybe I did it because I wanted to."

"Go back and do your thing. I got this!" She pushed herself away from me and made a shooing motion.

"Ok," I told her, grinning. "Let me know if you need anything. Does Owen need a bottle?" I asked for both of their benefits.

"Dayee, Owwwww—"

"Daddy's going back to work," Tina said sweetly. "You have mommy time." She scooped him up.

I turned at the door, ready to close it off between the office and living space and saw him bury his head in his mom's neck, his chubby little arms wrapped around her.

"My mama," he said, looking up enough to see me over the top of her shoulder.

I turned and walked back and put a finger on her shoulder near his head. "My mommy."

"My Mimi!" he said louder.

Tina laughed. "If you don't go now, you're going to be playing for an hour and then staying up all night."

"I'm going, I'm going. Sheesh. Hey, I'm going to leave the door open so the furry brigade of shenanigans can come back when they're ready," I told her.

"I'm going to close this, but I'll let one of the older ones come back if they want. I want to work with Owen and Sarge together while we're slow."

I shut the door behind me and heard her talking softly. I smiled to myself and went back to work. Because of Al scaring the crap out of me a couple years back, I'd changed everything to a Mac and tightened the security of my remote access software. He'd been trying to get back at me for a crack I'd made while he'd been locked up when a political rally had gone bad, and they'd arrested everyone. I'd told him to sleep with one hand over his butt and apparently, he'd mistaken my rare snark and wit for seriousness and spent a long, sleepless night waiting to get out in the morning.

It was funny now, but back then I'd been worried. I'd had a right to be worried as it turned out, but nothing was as it had seemed. I had got some hate email from a drunk in one of the western states a month later, but I'd wrote him back and it was funny, but I'd stayed in touch with him via email and he was embarrassed by all of that. I wiggled my mouse, then typed in the password. I turned off the baby monitor, then hit play on my phone that was docked and plugged into the Bluetooth speaker.

I often couldn't write to songs that have lyrics, not unless it's one I've heard so many times that it fades into the background. Instead, I love to listen to video game soundtracks, or acoustic versions of songs I know. Sometimes I risk my man card and pop in some Lindsey Stirling and listen to some gamer covers on violin and a synthesizer. It took the buzz of outside life away and soothed the part of my brain that acted like an overwhelming amount of white noise to my creative side.

Re-reading my last few paragraphs, I was getting back into the flow. My fingers were flying over the keyboard. I was reaching the inciting event in my storyline when my music cut off and my phone buzzed. I picked it up to see I had a phone call, from somebody I hadn't spoken to in a long stretch. Guiltily, I answered it.

"Hello?"

"Rick?" Veronica said, her words sobs.

"Veronica? Are you ok? What's wrong?" I asked,

shooting back from the keyboard, "Is it Al? What's wrong?" Panic rose in my chest at hearing her sobs.

"Al... he said... I need... you're..."

"Shhh," I said, "I can't understand you." The door to the office thudded hard.

I pulled it open and was almost tripped as all three dogs came barreling in. Ophelia stood up on her hind legs a moment before remembering she couldn't put her paws on me like that. Sarge wasn't so restrained, and I pushed him back as I almost lost the phone.

"Al said to ask you if you'd be his best man!" she said, crying loudly now.

I saw movement and Tina was rushing in the door with Owen in her arms, an alarmed expression on her face.

"Best man?" I almost shouted. "You're getting married?"

"Yes!!!!!!" she yelled into the receiver.

"Hell yes!" I called back.

"Thank you," she sobbed, and then it sounded like she dropped the phone and there was a click.

"I heard you yelling!" Tina said, bouncing Owen on her hip.

"Sorry, it was... Veronica. She sounded upset, hurt. Al just asked her to marry him, but only if I'd be his best man."

"Oh..." The tension drained from her face and was replaced with a smug smile.

"You knew?" I asked her, stunned.

"I knew he was going to, but I figured he chickened

out. I helped him pick out the ring two months ago. He bought it on the spot."

"Well, I'll be dipped in—"

"Little ears!" Tina chided.

Sarge barked happily and sat down between us, with Opus and Ophelia taking spots on the futon, looking at us expectantly.

2

RICK

"**D**ude, bro, thank you," Al said for the nineteenth time that day.

"You were my best man and you're my best friend. Just don't lock your knees and move your legs so you don't pass out when the music starts."

"You got the ring, right?" he asked me for the twenty-seventh time.

"No, I hocked it to the traveling circus that was passing through the parking lot, selling tickets to the freak show later on."

"That's not funny, dude," Al said under his breath as the conversation drifted to the pastor who was looking at me with a grin.

"Actually, I used it to pay off the bar tab last night after you—"

"I don't even remember last night," Al said. "Don't you go—"

I laughed softly and smacked him in the stomach,

interrupting him.

"It's right here on my pinky." I held my hand up.

He relaxed and then looked back at the pastor who nodded at him, smiling.

"We've all gone through it; it's the best gift you've ever given yourself and your wife-to-be," he said, meaning marriage, I assumed.

"Yeah, I just can't believe she said yes," he said.

That was when the music started.

"Don't lock your knees," I told him, watching him sway on his feet.

THE RECEPTION AFTERWARD WAS GREAT. I'D SAY IT WAS probably even more fun than mine, but I had also been nervous and overwhelmed by the turnout of people at my wedding, so I had mostly been trying to just survive. Tina dragged me to the dance floor while Ophelia watched from her spot under our table. Char had offered to watch Owen, and Opus and Sarge had decided to stay at home and watch over her and the baby. All in all, it was a good arrangement and we were at a FOE club only a few miles from the mini-storage.

I was starting to feel the effects of two drinks and exhaustion, but Tina wasn't quite ready to go yet. She pulled me onto the floor for one more dance when Shinedown's cover of Simple Man came on. I surprised myself by leading her on the dance floor for once and enjoyed the look of surprise. At the end, I kissed her hard.

"Dude, I didn't know you had any moves," Al said, walking up and putting his hand on my shoulder.

"Yeah, I don't think he danced like that at your wedding!" Veronica said.

"I think he's been holding back on me," Tina said, punching my shoulder.

"Maybe I watched some YouTube," I told them defensively.

"You about to split, man?" Al asked me suddenly.

Tina looked at me, her eyes a little glassy from drinking and having a lot of fun.

"I think so, it's almost two o'clock," I told him.

"Actually, we're ready to wrap it up too, but see... Veronica had this bet that you wouldn't make it as long—"

She punched him in the stomach gently, but it caught him off guard. Ophelia came out from under the table, sliding to a stop between Tina and I and looked up at Al, her head cocked to the side.

"She's not going to make Al cry," Tina said, smoothing her ears back.

Ophelia chuffed and then rubbed her head against Tina.

"I think I'm going to skate," I told him. "It's late, and the little tyrant is with a neighbor. I'm sure she don't mind, but he's going to wake up and—"

"You don't got to tell me, bro," Al said then pointed at Veronica's stomach, "we're about to find out how it goes... in like seven months?" he whispered, looking to her and she nodded.

Shotgun Wedding! I almost shouted the words, but

knew they were wrong and inappropriate. Besides, that was the beer talking.

"Congrats!" Tina and I chorused, "Jinx, you owe me a coke!" then we busted up laughing.

"I just hope getting married doesn't make me lame like these two," Veronica said, pulling Al by the shoulder.

He followed but she turned around and gave us a smile and mouthed, "Thank you!" We gave her a wave.

"I feel bad, shouldn't we stick around to help clean?" Tina asked.

"No, he's got a service for that," I told her, just as the music turned off.

"That's our cue," Tina said, pulling me by the hand.

I WOKE UP TO A SMALL FORM CRAWLING UP ON ME. I HEARD a soft snore beside me as Tina slept. My legs were pinned, and I could hear Opus also snoring from his dog bed by my side. The form was hairless and smelled oddly like milk, and I realized Tina must have pulled Owen into the bed from the crib. He'd been sleeping uneasy. He wasn't a fussy baby much, but he'd been teething lately. He had some molars coming in that were driving him bonkers... and causing us all to sleep fitfully.

"Dayee," he said softly, one small hand cupping the stubble on my chin before he rested his head in the crook of my shoulder.

"Owen, shhhhh," I told him softly.

He turned his head back and forth to get comfortable and then rolled fully onto his side. Sarge let out a sound in his sleep, and then he too was snoring again softly. I mentally went over my safety plan. I'd checked all the doors and windows twice. Even though I didn't tell Tina I was checking closets, we didn't keep ours closed unless Owen was running around, and I'd gone through them pretending to be looking for something. Then I'd made sure my pistol was in the keyless safe next to my bed. I felt on top of it, on the piece of felt and foam rubber I used to keep the pistol's finish clean when I was working the safe or reloading a magazine. It had been put away. In fact, I hadn't even carried it to the reception.

With Owen in bed with Tina and me, I went over everything. After a few minutes of listening to everyone sleep, I was convinced with my mental checklists that everything was safe. I closed my eyes in the darkness and was soon close to drifting. It had to be late night or early, early morning, but I wasn't for sure. All I knew was everyone was here and in the room with us, if not on the bed. Opus no longer wanted to sleep on the bed with us, but Ophelia had no problems taking his place. She'd become like glue to me. It was funny, when I'd first met Opus, he'd taken to me quite well, and Tina had accused him of being traitorous.

I think Ophelia realized that Opus had been just keeping me happy and it was her job to watch over me now. She sure acted like it and never let me forget that she was on the job, even if she didn't talk to me as much as Opus. I still needed to learn her body language a bit, or she needed more Opus lessons.

A phone call in the dark had me almost shooting up, but I felt Owen's weight and held myself back.

"Tina," I said, patting her shoulder.

"I'm on it," she said sleepily.

I extricated myself from under Owen as she found the landline cordless phone and answered it.

"Hello?" she asked.

I waited, but it sounded like Charlie Brown's teacher was on the other end of the line.

"Oh no... yes, yes... Don't you worry, Annette."

I sat up and snapped on the light, making all of us squint and causing Ophelia to roll off the bed in an undignified flop. She huffed her displeasure.

"What's going on?" I asked sleepily, pulling a pillow to block Owen from rolling off my side of the bed.

"It's Bud," she said, one hand over the phone.

"Don't you worry, we'll be right up. Uh huh... I know, you just have to... yes. I know you are. I love you too. I'll see you in a few hours," Tina said with tears in her eyes. "Yes, no, no don't... You... Trust me, we'll be there. Uh huh. I promise we'll drive safe. See you soon."

I was already adjusting the running mental list that went through my brain like the green letters flashing across the programmer's screen in the Matrix movies.

"How bad?" I asked her.

"They took him by ambulance. His heart stopped. She's waiting to hear from the surgeon," Tina said, walking over and sitting on my lap.

Opus got up and stretched as Tina wrapped her arms around me. Bud. He'd cheated death, and by all accounts should have died when he'd had his stroke two years ago. Now he was... was he dead? I wanted to cry too, and I rested my chin on top of her head and held the tears back. Opus walked over and put his head on both of our legs and let out a low whine, a mournful sound.

"He knows," Tina said, starting to sob.

"He can understand people," I told her, our short-hand on how he understood English.

"I... I told her that we'd—"

"I know. We need to get Owen changed, pack the diaper bag, probably a week's worth of diapers and wipes... I've got go bags in the van, but we need more clothes."

"We left clothes in War Wagon," Tina said, turning her head to look up at me.

"Yes, but we'll need some warmer stuff. I think we just left jeans and t-shirts."

"You don't mind?" she asked me.

"Hell no," I told her and then stopped as Owen made a sound.

We both cringed and looked, but the little tyrant let out a soft burp and cuddled into the pillow where I'd just been laying.

"What time is it?" I asked her.

"Almost 3am," Tina said.

"Half hour to pack, we're mostly loaded, have food at the RV... water?" I asked her.

"We can always fill our containers up there to save time," Tina said. "Bud and Annette said if we ever need-ed..." She started sobbing again, and I pulled her close.

Ophelia belly crawled across the bed, careful not to disturb Owen, and rolled on her side. She put a paw on Tina's leg. She looked down and smiled, despite the tears. Sarge, by this time, had woken up as well, but he sat at the door, looking a little confused by what all was going on.

"Ok, let's get it all going. I'll do the baby furniture if you want to get his clothes and diapers all set."

"I can," she said, steel in her voice, as she slid off my lap and onto her feet.

"I just hope we have enough time—"

"We can always pray," Tina said.

With that, I went and started tearing down the Pack-n-Play under the watchful gaze of the dogs.

"Sarge is sick, real bad," I told Opus, who was eye to eye with me.

Opus chuffed, then put his wet nose behind my ear and gave me a gentle lick. He knows, he understands. This, of course, got Ophelia's interest and she came over and tried to see what Opus had been up to. I finished the Pack-n-Play and then put it on top of the changing table, so I could get clothes out of the closet.

3

OPUS

Opus was confused at first, hearing the second name of the old human he liked. He knew his humans had to be talking about him because he could hear the old human's mate speaking. She sounded upset, and that made something in him ache almost as much as the old bullet wound that he would bite and itch at when the water fell from the sky and bright lights lit up the night with a sound like his human's guns.

He could see sorrow and fear in the faces of both, and saw the littlest human pup still sleeping. Knowing he was needed, he walked over to Rick and stuck his nose in his neck and gave him a comforting lick, then turned to the rest of the pack he ruled over. Using body language and almost sub-audible vocalizations, he let his mate and pup know that his humans needed tending to, and he thought they were going to be on the move. Maybe even up to where the evil squirrel army lived. Opus was unsure if the squirrels would be out in this cold, but as long as he could keep an eye on his humans, he might get a chance to chase one down.

The little brown things with big rear legs were easier to catch and far more abundant, but Opus remembered the mocking chitter as acorns rained down on him after his jaws closed on a squirt of fur that had just escaped.

He shook his head, seeing Rick putting the human pup's gear up, and focused. He was so tired, but he knew it was time to sleep soon again. Sarge pup almost tripped up his human woman, Tina, and he gave him a low growl and a nip near the back leg. Sarge spun, but saw he wasn't playing. Instead, Opus followed Rick out of the room to the front door, and his mate Ophelia followed. She was younger, but never missed an opportunity to try and make Opus jealous of the human she had adopted. She was trying to help him now as he wrestled the door open.

"Ophelia, no," Rick said, pulling the end of the Pack-n-Play out of her jaws.

Opus sneezed in amusement, and Rick locked gazes with Opus and rolled his eyes. Ophelia let go, and Opus chuffed to her. She sneezed back. With a sigh, he shot out the door after Rick. The screen door hadn't banged shut yet, and he heard two bodies hit it and the scrambling of paws to match his.

"Bud had a heart attack, or a stroke or..." Rick told them as he got the side door open to the big green vehicle Opus loved to ride in. In it, his humans carted him around like the king he was.

Opus let out a whining note of concern and got in. His usual spot was split in half with a large contraption that held the smallest human pup, called Owen, in place.

He got in on the other side as Rick slid the baby cage behind the seat.

"You going to stay in here or come on back in?" his human man, Rick, asked.

Opus laid down next to the big seat, making himself fit.

"Ok, I'm going to leave the door open. Not sure I can leave these other two goofballs alone out here. You guys go potty, it's going to be a long ride."

Sarge let out a happy bark and started wagging his tail so hard he almost fell over in excitement over the word 'ride'. Opus let out a sigh and looked over at Ophelia. She'd found something interesting by the fence to sniff and though he was tempted, he sat there. He would go investigate before more packages and the little human were loaded. For now, sleep. Dream. Go to the place where his side didn't ache, and the bad men didn't keep him from protecting the humans he loved.

"RICK, YOU KNOW... THIS WAS GOOD PRACTICE ON HOW long it takes us to bugout," Tina said quietly.

"I know," Rick told her. "I just worry that we took too much time—"

"It's ok, we haven't heard back from Annette. No news is good news," Tina interrupted.

Opus shifted, feeling relaxed and more awake than he had earlier. He yawned and slid off the bed, barely missing his pup. Sarge let out a loud yawn, complaining about being woken up, but Opus ignored him and pushed his way to the front between his humans. He got his ears scratched by the woman and laid his head on her leg, swaying with the movements of the big green van.

"We're almost there, buddy," Rick told him, adding a hand to his back, scratching in the spot that made his bad leg dance.

He couldn't help it, it was sore, but it felt good and soon his leg was thumping, inches from his mate's head. She let out a moan and then moved to jump up in the spot Opus had occupied. He decided to sit.

"Actually, this is our exit," Tina said.

Opus leaned against the seat with the coming movement of the vehicle and waited. Soon he would see the old couple he loved to visit so much.

4

RICK

We'd left both Ophelia and Sarge in the van for the time being. I'd unrolled two of my sleeping bags and neither of the dogs had had a problem burrowing inside of them to warm up. Tina and I had gotten out of the house in record time and while she'd gotten the baby unhooked from his car seat, I had gotten the other two dogs ready. I'd put their bowl down and added half a bottle of water. Both just looked at me like they were upset that they had to stay behind. I understood that, and I probably would have taken Ophelia in with me if it wasn't for Sarge. He wasn't as trained and polished yet.

Opus, on the other hand, had been volunteering with Tina in hospitals and she had a special harness with tags and paperwork showing that he was a certified therapy dog. I could see he was getting older by the way he moved. The bitter cold must be hell on his old injury, or he was too stiff. In a way, it was heartbreaking to see him slowing down. But I'd slowed down a little bit myself. Not the writing so much as mentally. I was now an adult. Married, with a baby man.

"Hurry," Tina said.

"I need to figure out where—"

"I know where to go," Tina said, Owen in her arms.

We hadn't brought the stroller in with us; Tina had grabbed the little tyrant, and I'd snagged the diaper bag. I had the leash stuffed in the pocket of my coat, but Opus wasn't leaving Tina's side.

"We need to go to 302," Tina said to the guy sitting behind the counter of the ER intake area.

"I... family?" he asked.

"Yes," Tina lied, though it was a small one.

"Go ahead," he said and hit a button somewhere under the desk.

The door buzzed, and Tina already had it open.

"Ma'am... never mind. I see his vest," he said as we both darted through, following in Tina's wake.

Opus chuffed, then whined.

"I know, buddy," I said, power walking to keep up with her. "We're all worried about Bud."

He let out another whine and went ahead of me a bit to keep up with Tina. I worried that she was going too fast while holding the baby and that if Opus got under her feet... But that didn't happen. She stopped at an elevator and pushed the button for up.

"How do you know this place so well?" I asked her.

"The last time. Same layout, same floors. Annette gave me the room number, but I don't know if he's in there yet."

"Oh, I hadn't realized he had a room. Maybe it's—"

Annette stepped off the elevator, her head down. Tears streaked her face, and she walked right into me. I dropped the diaper bag and caught us both before we could tumble down.

"Sorry, I—"

She looked up and saw me. She started sobbing and wrapped her arms around my chest. Tina had turned, and I saw something in her break as a tear fell down her cheek.

"Bud?" I asked.

"It was his time," she said between sobs.

I looked around and saw a bench about ten feet back and made a head nod. Tina nodded back.

"Opus, with me," she said before scooping up the dropped diaper bag.

"Gammy!" Owen shouted cheerfully.

"Hi there, Master Owen," Annette said, wiping her eyes.

"THEY GOT HIS HEART RESTARTED IN THE AMBULANCE. THEY think he was in a coma, but he didn't survive the operation," Annette said after her third cup of coffee and an hour of sitting on a hard bench. We'd since moved to the cafeteria, but she'd been too upset to do much talking until now. Her eyes were red, but she kept making faces at Owen once in a while and he'd get a grin out of her.

"I'm so sorry," Tina said for the hundredth time.

Annette was sitting between Opus and Tina with

baby Owen walking and crawling all over the spot we'd staked out in the cafeteria.

"I... I'm sorry, I didn't mean to dump this all on you guys. I just—"

"Bud was like a father to me," I told her. "I just wish I had visited more."

"He knew and appreciated all of it," Annette said, reaching over and patting my hand.

"I just..." Tina started.

"It's weird. Doctor Brett said he never should have survived the last time, but he did. We knew from that moment on that his time was short. Heck, his COPD was getting worse." She paused to take another sip of the industrial grade sludge the hospital claimed was coffee. "But knowing it was coming and thinking I had everything in my mind..."

She put her head down. Owen took the opportunity and pulled at a lock of her hair, oblivious to what had caused her to lean over.

"Gammy," he said, pushing himself further between Opus and Annette. "Gammy sad?" He asked in baby speak, though everyone could understand.

She reached down and pulled him into her lap. He let out a surprised squeak and then leaned in close, putting his head on her neck. I saw one eye looking my way, and I gave him a sad smile. He opened and closed his tiny hand. An Owen wave. Tina caught my gaze, and there was something in her eyes that I could only identify with as a feeling of great loss. I felt it too. Annette wrapped my little guy in both arms and hugged him back.

"I'm sad right now, Bubba, but I won't be forever.

Being able to hear you talk so clearly is helping me cheer up though."

"Owwwwwwwwwwwn," he said wiggling, "yuce."

She lowered him, and he came over my direction. I had the diaper bag and was feeling inside the insulated pocket and found one of several cups Tina had packed. I handed him the cup and he sat down and leaned back, sipping.

"I wonder how much he realizes is going on around him?" Tina asked, probably trying to distract Annette and herself from the sadness that was going on around them.

"I bet almost all of it," Annette said. "And after that hug, I think I'm feeling better."

She got to her feet, careful not to step on the little man. Opus turned and sat up, his head cocked to the side.

"You too," Annette said, rubbing his head.

"I'm going to go talk to somebody in charge," Annette told us. "I don't know what happens next."

"Want some company?" I asked her.

"Teenky!" Owen said, suddenly putting his cup down and pushing himself to his feet.

"What's stinky?" Tina asked.

The little tyrant snickered.

"Ok, I'll take diaper duty. How about you go with Annette and I'll catch up in a few?"

"Oh you don't have—"

"We love you like family. If you need us, we're here to help," Tina said, "I just need to call Char and ask her to manage the shop today, and I might as well take Opus outside and let the other yahoos out."

"Call me if you can't find us," I told her Tina.

My phone buzzed as Annette was signing a form. I looked.

All done. Dogs are restless. Where R U?

First Floor, almost done. Meet you in atrium?

KK

"Is that Tina?" Annette asked, her voice rough with emotion.

"Yeah, sorry," I said, pocketing my phone.

The funeral arrangements had been decided a long while back after Bud's first scare. A quick phone call to them would get the rest of the ball running from here on out.

"No, it's ok. I'm just glad you were here. I'm not sure..."

Her words trailed off and the administrator gave her a gentle pat on the hand. "I'm sorry for your loss," he said simply.

She nodded then stood. I followed, and we headed out.

"I'm going to be hearing that a lot, aren't I?" she asked me as we entered the atrium, leaving the small office behind.

"I think so," I told her. "How about we get you home?"

"That would be good. I rode in with the ambulance..."

"We've got this," I told her. "You can ride with us. Tina or I can help you make the arrangements."

"Talking about me?" Tina asked, and I felt a furry head push its way under my hand.

I scratched Opus's ears and realized Tina had seen us

27

first and had let Opus get my attention. My furry buddy let out a low groan of pleasure.

"You bet," I told her, "we're going to give Annette a ride back."

"Of course we are," Tina shot back.

Opus left my side and walked around and rubbed his head on Annette's hip, turning it like he was scratching his ear on her leg. She smiled and reached down to give him a pet.

"I know, buddy," she said, "I'm going to miss him too."

"Zaaaaab!" Owen said loudly, making all of us grin.

Opus chuffed, and Tina saw me looking at her and she grinned. It was funny when people started cluing into a dog's body language, but now wasn't the time to start talking about it. Seeing Annette smile was worth it to me to keep my trap shut.

"What was he trying to say?" Annette asked.

"I don't know," Tina said, "but he was pretty empathetic about it."

5

TINA & OPUS

Tina let Rick go with Annette inside her house to get the fire going. She'd taken Sarge and Opus with her and Owen to War Wagon. She'd learned all the systems and had no problem getting the pilot lit. With how much propane they'd gone through the last time they were snowed in, they'd learned to keep the big tank behind the shed topped off at the end of the season. In theory they could leave the pilot light lit, but as they had found out, motorhomes build up moisture easily.

"Dadadadadadada," Owen suggested from the bouncer Tina had put him in as a quick baby containment system that had they left behind from the summer.

"He's going to be a little bit, but won't be long. I don't think Annette is going to grieve for Bud while he's around. She's a tough one."

"Dargy!" Owen shot back, pointing at the younger shepherd.

"Are you trying to say Sarge or doggy?" Tina asked him.

"Dargy!" he said and busted up in giggles, pumping his legs up and down, making the motorhome floor shake.

Sarge, hearing his name, went over to Owen and cocked his head to the side, then leaned in and licked the baby on the face. Giggles turned into shrieks, and he took a step back and sat down on his haunches, looking at Opus, who was suddenly interested.

"You called him over," Tina said, turning to make sure the fridge was turned on and not running on propane. It worked on both propane or electricity, and the RV was plugged in.

Opus let out a groan, and Tina looked up to see Rick's big van coming down the driveway. Rick had dropped them off at the RV and taken Annette back. The wood must have been laid out and ready to go. Sarge, or Bud, to make things less confusing, hadn't liked using the fireplace and only did in the worst of winter. Tina felt a pang of sadness and wondered who would chop and haul wood.

"Dayeeeee!" Owen yelled as he bounced and pointed out the big window.

"That's your daddy," Tina said, smiling.

It was warming up in the RV with the furnace going full blast, so Rick was taking his coat off as he opened the door, letting Ophelia bounce in before he came in himself.

"It's cold out there," he told her.

Ophelia did what the other two dogs had done; run

from one spot to another, smelling everything, before coming back.

"How's Annette?" Tina asked him.

"Good. I got the fire going and made sure both our numbers were handy. Were you able to get ahold of Char?"

"Yes, she'll post a note on the door. It's coming into the slow season and her living so close…"

"It makes sense. I…"

"I know," Tina said, sensing his mood change and his smile falter.

"I just wish—"

"Me too. We never have enough time, do we?" Tina asked.

"I think when you're in love, there's never enough time," Rick told her.

Ophelia chuffed, then walked over to the bouncer and used her rear end to push Sarge out of the way and sniffed Owen's neck, then gave him a lick. He squealed and pushed her head back from him. She chuffed and backed up and laid down in front of him. Opus grumbled and Sarge's tail was going so hard he was bouncing almost as hard as Owen.

"I think you're right," Tina said, stepping forward into his arms and giving him a hug.

Opus whined and pushed himself between the two of them. Ophelia usually would have done the same, but she was watching the baby and barely paid attention to the older humans.

"Bud didn't have a ton of firewood cut. I'm going to go back and get that going if Annette isn't sleeping."

"We can hold down the fort. What are you thinking about dinner wise?" she asked, wondering what she should pull out from the shed to whip up into a meal.

"Whatever you want," Rick told her. "I'm going to check on things outside, check the locks, then walk back up and see if there's some stuff I can haul. Kind of put off making too much noise. I don't think she slept at all."

"No, probably not. I'll make sure she has a plate made up. Think she'd like to come down the trail a bit for dinner?"

"I can ask," Rick said, giving her a quick peck on the cheek.

"Opus, you want to come with me when I haul wood?"

Opus let out a bark and got up, his tail wagging.

OPUS FOLLOWED HIS ADOPTED HUMAN CALLED RICK. HE was moving far slower than he usually did and didn't take the big green van that Opus liked to ride in. Still, the chill air carried scent, and he could tell that somewhere close was a rabbit and a bunch of the evil squirrels. He was wary, but he knew he couldn't leave his human's side until he was for sure that—

A black squirrel darted across the driveway and Opus was off like a shot. His human called encouragement. Opus' lungs seemed to expand, and he ignored the pain in his rear leg and let his frustration and inaction out in one epic chase. The squirrel had started on the ground but had darted, trying to climb a smaller sapling. It tried to leap to a larger tree, but Opus sprung into the air. He caught it, like he would a frisbee or the ball that his human Rick liked to throw for him. The squirrel was wildly trying to get away, but being as careful as he could, he brought it back to his human. Rick's face was one of shock. He held his hand out and Opus opened his jaws. The squirrel was off like a shot. Opus chuffed and sneezed, trying to get the taste out of his mouth.

"You finally got one," Rick said, patting his head.

Opus looked up at him and chuffed, happy that he had shown his human that he had always been capable of catching them... but also pleased that the ones he did battle with and let loose often went back to their demonic hordes and warned them to stay away from his woods.

"I thought you always ate what you caught?" Rick asked him, starting to walk again.

Opus was limping slightly from age, arthritis, and behaving puppy like again, but he walked proudly with his human. Once again, he'd proved that he was willing and capable of protecting the people he had adopted. That was when he saw the rabbit.

6

RICK

I smiled as Owen sat in Annette's lap. Tina had let him help get dinner ready and they'd taken the entire pot of spaghetti over to her house. She'd set out the table and they'd started eating. Owen had insisted on sitting in Gammy's lap, and I wasn't going to tell him no unless she did or couldn't.

"He's going to get you orange from the sauce," Tina said for the third time.

"I'm not worried," Annette said, "I've had a good cry and a nap this afternoon. When I woke up, I realized it's little things that I remember the most. Little things like the joy of having a little boy sit in your lap, how your pack of dogs terrorizes the tree rats around here. Little things like knowing..." Annette paused and took a deep breath, "...like knowing friends and family are willing to help."

"I'm honored you think of us like that," I told her truthfully.

"Don't you get me started, I'll bust you in the chops," Annette said suddenly.

I hung there with my jaw open for a second, and then Tina and her began laughing at the same time.

"You channeled Sarge," I said, finally getting it.

"If I was channeling Sarge, I'd be talking about pulling your... No, I can't, little ears," she said, laughing.

I grinned and shook my head. Annette had made garlic bread by buttering slices of bread and putting garlic powder on it. I'd done this plenty of times with Al before I'd met Tina, but maybe Annette was right; it was the little things. They were good, they were honest, and each represented a happy memory.

"You know, I think I'm going to call the funeral home in the morning. The hospital administrator said he can even make the call if they don't hear from them in a few days."

"I can call if you want," Tina said.

Her voice was soft, but she seemed to radiate confidence. That was how she was usually, but there were still moments, especially after the nightmares involving Moab, that would sometimes momentarily shake her. She'd decided she'd never be a victim again and had gone out and gotten her own CPL, and on top of her workout routine of running, she had added self-defense classes. For the last six months, she'd been working to get her body and confidence in peak condition. She called it losing her baby pouch, but I think it had more to do with building her confidence.

I knew I still had issues of confidence. I'd been kidnapped, beaten, and almost killed by a childhood friend. After the media uproar had died down from that, I'd been quietly going to therapy. As a deeply introverted guy, I had few people I trusted so much. I mean, everything I thought or felt, Al already knew, but he was so laid back I didn't think he could have helped much. I never really believed in it much until I realized that sometimes, it was the self reflection and quiet conversations with somebody who understood what I'd gone through that won me over.

I'd failed. I'd failed as a man and a husband. I hadn't protected Tina and Opus when they'd needed me, and at the core of all of that was guilt. The therapist and I had danced around this issue until I had come to the realization that, in hindsight, there was very little I could have done.

"I'll call them in the morning. It's... Bud and I thought this was happening two or three years ago. Again, when he had his surgery. Now that it's actually happened... it hurts, it hurts bad," she said, a tear falling from her eye to hit Owen's mass of blond curls, "but I think I've come to terms with this. Now I'm just following through on a plan we'd figured out already."

"Gammy eat delicious?" Owen said, holding a fork up straight over his head.

"I... His hair—"

"Got it," Annette said and leaned over and took the bite before the spaghetti could drop into Owen's hair.

He giggled and started loading it up again when the house phone rang.

"I've got him," I said, reaching over and grabbing Owen from her.

Opus got up and chuffed, bringing both Ophelia and Sarge to their feet from where they'd been napping in front of the fireplace.

"I'll be just a moment," Annette said, shuffling toward the kitchen.

I heard her answer, and Tina reached over and pulled Owen's plastic plate over in front of me.

"Dayeeeee, I bubba?"

"You want your bottle?" Tina asked.

"Bubba!"

"I guess he's ready for a drink," I told my wife.

"Me too." She pinched my leg before reaching into the diaper bag and pulling one out.

"Yeah, I guess me too, but not a bottle," I said with a grin. "Anything stronger than a beer will have me snoring."

"Same here. I feel like we've been running on adrenaline and I'm now..."

"Crashing," I finished, watching as Opus padded into the kitchen.

Ophelia and Sarge followed, but stopped in the living room so they could watch the archways. I marveled at their behavior. Opus had sensed that Annette had needed him and Ophelia and Sarge had gotten in a position where they could watch the doorways and listen in.

"We've got a good pack," Tina said, noting my gaze.

"Yeah, except the hairless one," I said, patting Owen. "He's got to learn how to communicate better," I teased.

"The hairless one," Tina said, her nose wrinkling up at my word usage, "already understands their body language. I think you're just the slow one to catch on."

"Me? Slow?"

Tina smirked at me and Owen caught her smile and smiled back. Annette finished her bit and then put Owen down. He wobbled for a second then started walking toward the dogs. He'd never been near the fireplace without one of us, but he knew the basic concept. Opus lifted his head and watched my son walk his way.

"Opus, good!" Owen said, holding his hands out.

Opus stood and Sarge shook himself to his feet just as Owen flopped on the ground in front of them both.

"Nice?" he asked, offering his hands.

Opus started licking one hand and then Sarge started on the other one. He giggled and both dogs sat back down, keeping themselves between the fire and the baby man.

"He just wanted to get his hands cleaned," I told Tina.

"Having you here, all of you... it means a lot to me," Annette said, walking back into the room.

"We're here as long as you need us," Tina said.

THE FUNERAL WAS A SOMBER AFFAIR. WITH EVERYTHING IN order, he was cremated and there was a small ceremony. Most of the town showed up, which meant maybe a couple dozen people I recognized and most I didn't. I sat in the back with Opus and the little man for most of the service. I'd said my goodbyes and had been visiting with Annette when I could. I'd remembered to bring my recorder, so I was getting a lot of things dictated when the silences became unbearable and I needed to walk.

"You ok?" Tina asked me, after having stood up front with Annette for a bit.

"Yeah," I told her, "why?"

"It's just that you're so quiet, so contained..." she said, brushing my hair aside on my forehead.

"I... I'm going to miss him, but I don't think he'd want me to be sad and upset that he's gone. Part of me feels that, but most of me is looking at this and holding the little man kind of brings it home to me."

"Don't dwell on it too long, we need you," Tina said then bumped me with her hip.

"Mamamamamamamamamamamama—"

"Ok, I got you," Tina said, grabbing Owen, who'd opened his arms, holding them up in the universal *pick me up* gesture.

"Opus, you want to go up with me?" I asked him.

He chuffed and then rubbed his head against my leg. Most of the town folk recognized him and I would have brought in Ophelia also, but she was needed to keep Sarge from chewing up everything in the RV while we were gone.

"Want me to come up with you?" Tina asked.

"No, that's ok. Hey, that smell—"

"You waited until he went to me to notice he needed a diaper?" she asked, one eyebrow arching.

Opus sniffed, then sneezed. It sounded suspiciously like he was calling bullshit, but his tongue was hanging out and he was holding himself at an easy smile. I wished I could be so flippant, but I realized seeing everyone here around me that maybe this was what having a family about was like. In the end, we share and remember. We love, we live, and when we pass, the cycle keeps repeating.

"Down?" Owen asked, very clear in his question.

"Not yet, you're stinky," Tina told him and kissed his forehead.

"Teenky, Dayee!"

"I'll be right back," I told Tina.

"Take your time," she said then leaned over and kissed me on the cheek.

"Opus buddy, you ready?"

He chuffed.

I walked up to the front. Instead of a casket, there were three easels set in place, with a shelf and an urn in the middle. Each of the easels held a picture board. They were arranged from right to left in what looked like Bud's entire life. From the grainy picture somebody found of him as a kid to the first day of boot camp, his head shaved, and looking like he was two days after a major fist fight. Pictures of him and Annette, their wedding, their son. Lots of pictures with Bud and his son.

The third board had me almost choking up. It was a picture of me in front with Bud directing the action. It was when I'd dragged some of the cut trees into the area where he cut and split his firewood near his outdoor smoker. I grinned and saw that there were a ton of pictures of him holding baby Owen, of our families at the diner having biscuits and gravy, extra bacon. Puppy Sarge under the table with Ophelia and Opus.

Opus made a whining sound and leaned into me. I looked up to see Annette standing there. Her cheeks were dry, but I could see she was getting tired.

"You ok?" she asked me.

"The real question is, how are you?" I shot back, avoiding the question.

"I'm doing good, I guess, but—"

"It's because you're so quiet," Annette said, petting Opus between the ears in the spot he liked.

He couldn't help it, the tail started wagging and the leg lifted, and he started thumping it on the ground as she hit his spot. I saw her smile and at that moment I decided that the thing about funerals I'd always understood it, was wrong. This wasn't a last goodbye. This was a celebration of the life lived, of sharing memories. It started to hit me funny, so I leaned in and gave her a quick hug.

"You two getting going soon?" Annette asked.

"When I've gotten enough firewood split, then I'll—"

"I've got a firewood delivery coming. Bud was too cheap to pay for it, but despite him being a tight ass penny pincher, I can afford the luxury. I meant *today*. You going to stick around for the luncheon?"

"Of course," I told her. "We were going to stick around for a couple of days more at least."

"You know, you don't have to do that," Annette said. "Like I said, I'm going to miss him, but we saw this coming. For a long time."

"I know," I said quietly.

"Plus, I've got a confession to make," Annette said, leaning closer.

"Yeah?" I asked, our voices were barely a whisper, and people were giving us room.

"With you two so close, I can't sneak my boyfriend in; you're cramping my style, kid."

I stepped back, stunned, and then she busted up laughing. After picking my jaw up off the ground and making sure it was seated properly I joined in. People stopped and stared, but we didn't care. Opus barked loudly, happily, and spun in a circle. I knew he wanted to get up on his back legs and stand up and dance with us, but he was too dignified to do that.

"You ok?" Tina asked.

"We're cramping her style," I said, hiccupping the words out.

"What's that mean?" she asked, bewildered. Owen was now wearing a different onesie shirt, evidence of something nefarious.

"I don't know what he's talking about," Annette said, turning away to wipe her eyes. "You two really should get going though. Don't worry about me, and for all that's holy, how about you two get a quick honeymoon in somewhere?"

"Why the sudden change in subject?" I asked her.

"Because I realized this is exactly what Bud would have wanted of us. Heck, you pick someplace nice and warm, maybe I'll join you two and watch Master Owen some!"

I put my arm around Tina and hugged her close to me. Owen made a frantic sound, and I snatched him out of his mom's arms.

"What you want?" I asked him.

"Dayee, my barge n fee n oppy?"

"You catch that?" I asked Tina who shook her head no.

"He said he wants his Sarge, Ophelia and Opus," Annette said, making us both look at each other.

"Yes, doggies," Owen said promptly, pointing down.

I knelt, and Opus put his nose in Owen's neck, sniffed, then licked him across the side of the face. He squealed and started giggling, which prompted more giggles. I hated to break it up, but it looked like there was somebody waiting anxiously to talk to Annette and they were looking oddly at the vicious furry missile near devouring a toddler with his tongue.

7

RICK

"Do you really think that she'll want to come?" Tina asked.

"I don't know," I told her, "but if she wants to go on this cruise with us, it'll be a good time for her. If not... well, they have childcare there."

"I don't know how I feel about going without the dogs," Tina said.

Ophelia let out a low growl that made Tina scrunch up her face. We'd been home for a couple days and Tina had immediately gone to the task of looking places up. She said it was more for her, but we both knew it was a white lie. We'd avoided going on vacation since the wedding and had avoided traveling on our honeymoon. We both had been dealing with the mental and physical scars of our abduction. Now though, the thought of us going somewhere with the dogs and the baby didn't make my blood run cold.

"You getting lippy with me, Miss Ophelia?" Tina said,

adopting the baby voice she did when she was trying to egg on one of the dogs.

Ophelia barked sharply and then sat on her haunches, her tail wagging so hard I thought she was going to leave streaks of fur. Sarge came barreling into the room at her bark, and we both turned to watch as he scrambled across the tile. He was coming to check things out like he always did, but he didn't stop as swiftly as he ran or cornered. He barreled into me trying to run sideways.

"Oooof," I said, hitting the floor with my butt.

Both dogs immediately inspected me for damage, and one of them started licking me.

"Stop," I told them, putting my arms over my head.

"Dayeeeee!" Owen screamed from across the room.

I heard small feet scampering and then thirty pounds of lead launched itself onto my back, laughing and screeching with joy. I heard a big, deep bark and immediately everyone stopped, even Owen.

"It's ok, Opus, they weren't hurting Rick. Just playing," Tina said, walking toward him.

He sniffed her hand but stopped by me, and rubbed his head against my cheek before turning and hopping up on the couch.

"Somebody's got to be the mature one around here," I told Tina.

"Yeah, and that's me," Tina said, sitting down next to Opus.

"Meeeeeeeeee," Owen repeated and slid off me.

"I kind of want to go," I told her. "If we can find someplace down there to board the furry kids...?"

"I know... I've been searching for pet-friendly things, but so far I'm striking out."

"So what if we take it slow, drive down to Houston and then pick Annette up from the airport, we hop on a cruise and..."

"Why don't we all just fly?" Tina asked.

"Dayee go vroom!" Owen said simply.

"Yup, Daddy goes vroom," I agreed. "Plus," I said talking over his head, "I always like to be ready for anything, and I can't pack what I want for everything when I have to check baggage."

"You can't take all that stuff on the cruise!" Tina said. "Strict weapons policy, outside food and drink... Hell, they even have a dress code for the casino—"

"I was mostly kidding," I told her. "But I'd still rather drive. It gives us more options, and I know how wide awake you stay when we drive. Besides, it'll give us more options."

"We don't exactly have a great history of long road trips," Tina pointed out.

"We had the one incident," I told her. "Besides, if we don't drive, we have to keep the dogs boarded longer."

Tina bit her lip, and Opus rubbed his head against her thigh.

"What could go wrong on a cruise ship?" she asked me.

"Famous last words," I teased.

She grinned and nodded.

"Dayee up?" Owen asked, his toddler arms straight up in the air.

I snagged him and walked into the office. More and

more he was interested in anything and everything that I'd been doing. I'd started letting him come in and sit with me when I wasn't doing my writing sprints. Otherwise, I'd have to keep half an eye on him and half an eye on Sarge, who liked to chew still. It was the one habit that he'd yet to be broken of.

"Little man, we're going to look at places for the dogs to get babysat so we can go on a big cruise ship. How's that sound?"

"High five?" Owen asked, shifting so he was sitting on my left leg, his little chubby hands reaching for my keyboard.

"That sounds good to me too, buddy."

I woke up my Mac and typed the password in one handed as I held Owen from going over backward with my left. I hadn't been a huge Opera fan before, but after all the scares I'd had, I'd started using it. It had a built in VPN which made finding your IP address more difficult. On top of that, I'd subscribed to a service and they'd sent me another box to put in between my computer and the router. I'd started losing track of technology the more focused I'd become in my writing.

Owen and I worked on that until Tina walked in, her tablet in one hand and holding a phone to her ear with the other.

"Uh huh. Yeah, three German Shepherds. Two males. Uh huh, both of them are now. No, they're actually very well trained. Opus, my oldest, and Sarge's sire, is a working K9 and therapy dog. He's eight. Oh no worries, none of them are pet aggressive. Yeah, I think so. We have dates open from..." She looked at me, and I shrugged; we hadn't really planned a specific date yet. "Looks like we're open. Do you have any... Yes, that'll work perfect. Yeah, 48 hours for their Bordetella? I'll have to ask the vet and get records. Uh huh. Sure!"

Tina dropped me a wink and walked out. Owen wiggled, and I let him slide off my leg. He bumbled his way after her. There was a minor collision in the doorway as Opus and Ophelia came in and Owen bounced off one and into the other. Opus chuffed and sniffed at his head before getting on the futon behind me. Ophelia rubbed her head on Owen and then walked over and sat down next to me, putting her head in my lap. Owen toddled off.

"You two staying out of trouble?" I asked.

Ophelia's eyes changed a moment, her head turning and then she let out a soft chuff. Opus, of course sneezed, and I turned to point at him.

"You, sir, I expect more out of you," I admonished, teasing.

He chuffed and then sneezed at me again. Jerk.

"Ok, ok," I told them, listening to little feet heading toward the bedroom where I could hear Tina giving out her credit card information. "We've got to find us a trip. Sounds like Char is willing to make a little extra money. I think she and Detective Stallings are getting hot and heavy. I think she'll be the next one to go on a cruise," I teased them.

Opus stretched out and yawned deeply. I didn't blame him. Despite me getting older, I'd avoided slowing down. For him though, it was sort of painful to see the progression of him aging. He was in his senior years. I didn't blame him wanting a nap one bit. Heck, there were plenty of days I wanted one too.

"Bingo," I said, finding something interesting.

"I got a set of dates booked for the furry kids," Tina said, walking in with Owen on her hip. "They were a little apprehensive at first when I told them they should be kept together, but they remember the news story."

I cringed. There's a couple ways for a guy like me to get famous, and I wasn't comfortable with either. First was from notoriety of the kidnapping, and the second was because I was an author. One fed into another, and I won't lie, book sales had soared after the events in Wyoming and Utah as the television anchors put together the journey and trip. Hell, I'd turned down 60 Minutes. I'd avoided most of the press, and they'd finally decided to leave me alone. Mostly. That was another component in why we hadn't left for a vacation or elaborate honeymoon.

"Good, I think I found us a cruise," I told her, sliding the chair back.

She walked over and sat on my right leg. I put my arms around her as Owen looked across her arm at me and smiled.

"Yes, your mommy is still small enough to sit on my lap," I told him.

"And if I'm ever not too tiny?" She moved the mouse with her left hand, scrolling.

"I'll suffer in silence," I shot back.

"Good call," she said, then leaned back.

"This looks perfect," she told me.

Carnival Cruise Lines.

"Look at that," I said as Owen scrambled off of her lap and did the toddler walk to the futon.

"Owen?"

"No, it's half the price if we drive to Miami instead of Galveston."

"Oh yeah, that's weird. I haven't been to Florida much, just as a kid to see Mickey Mouse."

"Meeheee house?" Owen asked as he crawled up next to Opus and then sat back, bouncing off the back cushion of the futon without disturbing the half awake pooch.

"Not this time," Tina said. "And if we go down to Miami, we can avoid the southwest altogether."

She voiced the main reason why it had caught my eye. Texas was a long hike from Utah and probably another half a day to drive across it or better to get to Galveston, but it was too close. I was over it, but sometimes...

"That sounds good to me," I told her. "Four day or seven day?"

"It's entirely up to you," she said sweetly, leaning back into me.

"My mommy!" Owen said loudly, making Tina snicker.

"Don't worry, baby man, I'm not stealing her," I told him.

"How about a seven day?" I asked her. "I can drive it in a day or two, we're gone for seven and we can come back slow; maybe even hug the coast for a while?" I asked her.

"My, oh my. You want to get out and see the sights?" she said, turning.

Opus chuffed from his spot behind me, and Ophelia made a whining sound.

"Yep," I told her simply, "but looks like you better cancel the dog sitter in Houston." I poked her in the side. "We have to find somebody closer to Florida."

IN A WAY, PACKING FOR THE CRUISE WAS BOTH EASIER AND harder than just packing for the property up north to go visit War Wagon. For one thing, I usually brought up extra supplies to pack for the bugout up there. I'd made a pretty sizable stash here as well, but I had started keeping stuff in the van. That redundancy made things easier for me, but I worried it'd make me too complacent. Still, I put together a list as Tina coordinated with Annette and got the tickets booked for everybody. I threw it all on my card, despite Annette's protests. She and Bud had helped me out and had quite literally made me an offer I couldn't refuse on the land I'd bought. I almost felt guilty, but over time I'd realized that however it happened, they were wanting somebody to love and appreciate the area as much as they did. The solitude and quiet. Bud was a big time introvert like me, but for different reasons. Becoming second family to them was a happy bonus.

Tina got her and Owen's stuff packed, and I got on Amazon and ordered some new summer wear. In Michigan, October was cold and everything I had didn't fit. Since it was out of season, nothing local carried it. Tina had teased me, saying she'd gained the weight I'd lost. It was true on my part, I'd thinned out, but it was on purpose and with exercise. Something I'd been neglecting lately.

"Dayee, I wan bubye," Owen said as I went into the pantry.

"We're going," I told him. "When you wake up."

"Bye?"

"You bet," I told him. He leaned in close, his forehead brushing against my hip.

It took me a second before I realized that he was rubbing his head on my hip, much like the dogs did. When I picked him up, he did the same thing, only against my head or neck. Who had taught him the hug? The dogs, or was he the one who'd taught the dogs that? I rubbed his head affectionately and pulled out a full bag of dog food and the spare steel dishes. I'd have to fill up a couple of water jugs, but I was ready to go.

8

TINA & OPUS

Tina watched through half lidded eyes as Rick drove. He'd gotten her and Owen up at 4 a.m. He claimed that if they left right then they could avoid all the traffic snarls of Detroit, Toledo, and a couple other big cities. Everything, all but themselves, had already been packed. Rick had already let the dogs out, and they were waiting, with Sarge sitting on her seat.

Still, her heart soared in an excitement she hadn't felt in a couple years. This was a whole new adventure in a different direction. She knew things were going to be good, and she felt like bursting with every new word combination and sentence Owen made. She hadn't remembered feeling this whole and complete before.

The big van she called Rick's creeper van was comfortable though. The seats up front were comfortable and the suspension made sitting up front like being in a rocking boat or chair as they went across uneven pavement. Between them, Opus watched from next to Owen, with Ophelia on the other side on the bench seat. Sarge had tried to wedge himself on top of her to get his head out the window, but it was too cold and instead he'd picked the spot between the seats and was also snoring softly. Her eyes were getting heavy, even though she knew the sun was about to break across the horizon.

OPUS WOKE WITH A START. HE'D BEEN HAVING A DREAM about the squirrels again, and in it they had taken his humans. He was more of a superficial thinker and shrugged it off. He saw that his human, Rick, had some sort of headphones on. The rest of the van was silent except for the sounds of everyone else sleeping. Opus stood up and stretched. Rick caught the movement from the rearview mirror and put his hand back. Opus sniffed it for a treat, but finding none, he licked the hand. A reminder to make sure to send the sausage bites back next time, but his human felt the need for comfort.

Opus was used to long trips and remembered one he wished he could forget. This trip, though, was different. They weren't going north into the woods, the sun was on the wrong side, the way it was when they came back from the woods to the mini-storage. Except the smell was wrong. They were going a different way that he'd never gone, at least since he'd adopted this big family. The road blurred by, cars passing them with a burst of air that seemed to make the big van sway. His legs were used to this; he loved going for a ride with his older humans, and it didn't take him any thinking.

He looked over and saw the human baby, Owen, was asleep. He figured he should warn the humans in the front that he'd done something foul smelling in his sleep, but they didn't know how to listen to him. That was when he got an idea. He got down on the floor and then spun around in a circle, making a whining sound. Rick looked back in the rearview, and Opus whined again.

"You have to go to the bathroom?" Rick asked, pulling his earbuds off.

Opus scrambled to an excited attention, waking up Ophelia, who heard the word bathroom. She also hopped off the bench seat and was fighting to get in the middle, pushing against Opus' shoulder, waking Sarge up. The bark didn't only wake up the dogs. Owen started to cry, and the human Tina yawned and stretched.

"Where are we?" Tina asked.

"Not sure yet, pulling into a rest stop to let the critters out to water the lawns."

"Sounds good, I'm going to get Owen out, check his diaper, and get a bottle going," Tina said, still yawning.

Opus sat back, his tongue lolling out of the side of his mouth. Mission accomplished.

9

RICK

"Oh hey, aren't you that guy?" a woman asked, walking out of the restrooms with what had to have been her husband or boyfriend.

"I guess it depends on what guy," I told her, holding Sarge's leash tight while Opus and Ophelia sniffed and marked the trees near him on a longer lead.

Truth was, they were only leashed because of other people's fears and misconceptions.

"The author guy with the attack dogs?" she said.

"Oh yeah, I remember hearing about you. You're a local, right?" the husband piped up.

"Sort of, that was a couple years ago, but don't worry, these guys aren't attack dogs," I said, noting how the wife was suddenly wary.

Sarge got down on his belly and started crawling slowly toward her. He must have sensed that she was scared. That got Opus's attention and, without tangling the leads, both he and Ophelia started back, the reels winding up the slack on the springs. I grinned as the woman at first took half a step back and then a smile came across her mouth and she knelt down, offering her hand up. Sarge rolled onto his stomach and pawed at her hand playfully, trying to sneak a lick in.

"He doesn't look that dangerous," the husband said.

"It's the old guy, Opus here, you might have read about, and his lady friend, Ophelia. They were the ones who saved us," I said, kneeling as I got bumped in the side by Opus.

"Dayee!" I heard Owen's cry from behind them. I saw Tina's grin as she put Owen down, and he came bounding my direction. I had my hands full of leashes but that didn't stop the nearly thirty-five pounds of joy from trying to tackle me off my feet. Sarge rolled onto all fours and turned to inspect his little man. I grinned and handed Tina the lead for her pup.

"These guys are so beautiful," the woman said, running her fingers through Sarge's fur behind his head.

"They really are. Wicked smart too," Tina told her. "I think Opus knows something like two hundred commands—"

"And you can just talk to him, and he talks back."

"What?" the husband asked, skepticism in his voice.

"His name is Opus, ask him a question, or better yet..." I leaned closer and whispered to him.

Opus cocked his head sideways but didn't do anything else.

"Opus, your owner here tells me you like to wear a tutu and be a pretty, pretty little princess?" he asked.

Opus sneezed.

"Oh wow, he just called bullshit," the woman said laughing.

"Yeah, he's got a mouth," Tina said, taking Owen's hand. "He's got his way of saying yes and no, and I'm not quite sure if he manipulated us into stopping so I could change a stinky diaper."

"Teenky!" Owen agreed, giggling.

Opus chuffed and rubbed his head against my leg. I pet him, and he let out a grumble of pleasure. The woman took half a step back.

"Oh, he's just telling me that feels good," I told her, scratching faster, making his grumble higher in pitch.

It relaxed her, but she looked over my shoulder. Time to go?

"That's pretty interesting," the husband said, following everything we said.

Ophelia took a step forward and then sat down in front of the couple and put a paw up, putting it on his leg. He looked at me, and I was about to explain when Tina beat me to the punch, "That's Ophelia, she's introducing herself. You can shake her hand if you want, but she's just letting you know she thinks you're all right."

"You got all that?"

"It's a body language thing. For a long time, it was Rick, me, and Opus here. As you can see," she said, nodding to Owen and the other dogs, "our family unit grew a little bit."

"Someday, we hope to do the same," the woman said, rubbing her stomach unconsciously. "It was nice talking to you both and, Rick, keep writing!"

I gave a small nod and a wave. "They recognized me and the dogs from what happened..."

"It's bound to happen," Tina said told me. "More and more, the more books you write, the more well known you'll become."

"More like notorious," I grumbled, and Ophelia came over and rubbed her head against my leg.

"Let's get everyone loaded up and you can hit the head," Tina said.

"Sounds good."

We got back to the van and loaded everyone up, and I headed back inside. On my way out, I checked the map. Every rest stop in the country seemed to have the 'You are here' maps. I'd made good time so far. We didn't have to power through the trip though, not like we'd done out west. With three dogs, the baby, and Tina falling asleep, I'd be lucky to make the drive in three days. I'd planned for four or five. I did some mental math and saw I'd already be somewhere in Tennessee or Northern Georgia if I went at my old road trip warrior style. I just hoped to get two thirds of that, depending on how things went.

WE STOPPED FOR A LATE BREAKFAST, EARLY LUNCH, AND TO let the dogs out again. Owen was talking up a storm, and I was relieved that, on our first long trip, he wasn't fussy or screaming. He was a pretty easy going guy, to be fair. Sarge kept trying to goad Owen into dropping food, but Ophelia and Opus tried not to look at the french fries that Tina was feeding the baby man a few at a time.

"How far do we want to go tonight?" Tina asked.

"That's up to you," I told her. "And we can stay in the van or get a hotel room. Either way is fine with me, but we might have a harder time with three dogs."

"I hadn't thought about that," Tina said through a mouthful. "You have your big blow up mattress packed?"

I snorted, making Opus sit up from his bench in the van. I caught the movement from the rearview mirror and handed back a few fries.

"Hey! He can't eat that," Tina scolded me, but it was too late; he had scarfed them as soon as they were offered, and he was licking the salt off my hands.

Owen giggled and tried handing his fries over, but Opus turned his head, knowing better. Sometimes, I thought the training was more for the humans, it helped us bridge the communication gap. I'd been going with Ophelia for a couple years now. She'd bonded closely with me and often wouldn't leave my side, but her personality was a little different than Opus's. She would sit behind Tina instead of me, where Opus was, but I'd figured out it was so she could actually see most of me.

All the dogs loved on Owen, but I couldn't figure out which dog had claimed him yet. It was a toss up between Opus, who'd adopted all of us, but Sarge more and more was becoming glued to the baby man. I thought it was because he'd stayed with us when we'd given his litter mates to the breeder that Ophelia had originally come from. We could have sold them individually, especially with the pedigrees of the two O's, but we wanted the breeder to keep the bloodlines of them alive and going. They had quite literally saved our lives.

"Sorry," I told Tina after pulling my hand back, "it's not like he's doing CrossFit training."

"He's getting older though," Tina shot back, a hint of annoyance in her voice.

"So are we," I reminded her and reached over and put a hand on her arm.

"Yep, and you're older than me," she said and stuck her tongue out.

"So the dog can't have fries but the baby can?" I asked her.

"Hey, don't use that logic with me, you're setting a bad example." She smiled.

"There's an interesting stop along the way. It's not much of a side track but..."

"Side!" Owen shouted, and Opus let out a chuff.

"What were you thinking about?" Tina asked me.

"The Jack Daniel's Distillery is sort of on the way. It's just past Murfreesboro," I told her.

"Let me punch it up," Tina said and started playing with the GPS.

My phone dinged and although I usually tried not to look at it while I was driving, this time I did. I unlocked it and saw a text from Annette.

Don't text me back if you're driving. I'm almost all packed, and I had a load of wood delivered. I hired some of the younger town kids to come stack it. I know you were worried about that, but I think maybe all of us need this vacation.

"Annette?" Tina asked.

"Yeah," I told her, putting the phone back in the center console, "she says don't text and drive and she got the firewood situated. I think she's excited to come on vacation with us."

"Yeah... hey, that's a long bit to drive in one day isn't it?" she asked me, pointing to the new GPS readout.

"It might be. We could go as far as you want tonight and then maybe see if they have any tours open, first thing in the morning?"

"I like that idea better," Tina said. "Road trips make me sleepy."

I almost stuck my foot in my mouth but caught myself. Soon, everyone was sleeping or nodding off, leaving me in semi-silence. I got my recorder out and got my microphone ready. Out of self-consciousness again I looked around and although I could only hear snores from Owen, Tina appeared asleep. More than a few times I'd been dictating a story to have Tina hear me going and die of laughter. Although my wife absolutely knew what I was doing, hearing the words come out of my introverted mouth just made her get the giggles and threw off my game.

I had a story idea, one I had been playing around with since Utah. It was a prepper post-apocalyptic story about an outlaw prepper. He never tried to hurt people, but by letter of the law, he was an outlaw on just about everything he did day to day. Maybe it was time to start it up again.

"THAT WAS ACTUALLY KIND OF INTERESTING," TINA TOLD me as we walked out of the distillery.

"Too bad Lynchburg is in a dry county, huh?" I asked her.

"Daddy juice!" Owen said loudly and although I got a wry grin from Tina, I knew it annoyed her a little bit.

"It's definitely not Owen juice," I told him. "Hun, you ready to get back on the road?" I asked her.

"You better believe it."

10

TINA

Tina feigned sleep in the afternoon because traveling always made Owen sleepy on short trips, and it was turning out he enjoyed his waking moments as well. Tina listened and heard him snoring softly. Opus was behind Rick, staring out the window, always watchful. In such a short time things had changed dramatically, but she wouldn't trade her life for anything in the world. The entire writing process and the things Rick knew about publishing and the writing culture, she was getting used to. Saying all of that, though, she was always amazed at the stories he came up with.

She'd married him for his heart as much as his mind with zero regrets. Right now, she had her eyes closed and was listening to him *finally* start a story in another genre. She'd told him more than once that he didn't have to wait for them to fall asleep, but he'd told her that he'd bore them to sleep anyway. She chalked it up to insecurity and faked sleep for as long as she could, so she could listen in and let him get some work done.

That was one thing about the writer's world she'd learned through him. There's a 'churn' to things. Not a literal upheaval, but until a writer's career has taken off to the point they become a household name, the best way to get out there is to write more books, publish, and market. He had a knack for the marketing and research. He was a great storyteller, but it was how easy it came to him that amazed her. Her parents said much of the same when she told them about the eBay business she was starting with abandoned household items. The barn had been built using that money, and the property and mortgage she had taken out to buy the business from her parents had been paid off by the profits.

She didn't ask Rick about his money and he didn't ask about hers; she had always thought that it was gauche, even for husband and wife. They always had enough to do what they wanted...

"Go to sleep," Rick said.

"I am asleep, silly," Tina said and opened her eyes, grinning at him.

"No you're not, you're listening in."

"That's because you're not writing Paranormal Romance. This is a prepper story, isn't it?"

Rick nodded and smiled. "I wasn't sure I wanted to do one. The market is so volatile, but with the way the election went, the social unrest... I mean, it might be something hot to get into with the current timing."

"You do the market research, so you already know how it's going to do, right?"

"I do," Rick agreed. "The trick is to make the first book catch on and build my mailing list."

"Boring," Tina said and made a mock snore, turning her head.

Sarge bounced over Ophelia and tried crawling in her lap, looking for the sound. Tina laughed and pushed him back, telling him that there was no room up front for him on her lap. Opus chuffed, and Ophelia whined a bit.

"Where do you want to stop for the night?" Rick asked her.

"Hotel you mean?" he asked.

"Could be a hotel, campground, van, I really don't mind. We'll have another eight or so hours once we stop for the night I think, judging by little man and his moods."

"He's likely to keep us up all night, he's been sleeping so much," Tina told him.

"I know. I think he's probably enjoying all of this. He's a lot less talkative than normal."

"Hm... how about after the next rest stop I trade one of the furball's seats?"

Opus looked at her and then cocked his head to the right, his eyes boring into her. She caught Rick looking in the rearview mirror and grinning and caught Opus in the act of asking.

"Ok, Opus, you can have my seat next, but no hanging your head out the window. That's not dignified and a dog of your stature..."

"You're talking like he's Fitzwilliam Darcy," Rick interrupted.

"Yes, he's exactly like that. He's got his happy ending, and next rest stop he'll have my seat."

"Not if you take a turn driving," Rick said without looking.

"I can't drive this beast—"

"Oh malarkey," Rick countered. "You can drive War Wagon, you just pretend you can't. Remember?"

Tina was busted, and she knew it. "I'll take a turn if you want."

"No, I was just kidding. No worries," Rick told her.

"He probably thinks we can't hear him from the back-seat if he decides to dictate more," Tina told Opus, who chuffed his answer to her.

TINA SAW THE SIGN FOR A NATIONAL PARK AS THE SUN WAS starting to set. She and Rick decided that it would make a good spot to have dinner since most parks had a spot to use a grill. They had packed some bratwursts and potato salad with other stuff so they didn't get sick on road food before the cruise. Rick had remembered to pack half a bag of charcoal just for this purpose. They weren't surprised to find things exactly as they thought just inside the Florida border.

"Ohhhhh, this is so pretty," Tina told nobody.

"It is. I'm going to get out and stretch. We parked down from the public bathrooms a little bit, if you want to go I can change Owen and let him run around until it's time to get the grill going."

Sarge started barking loudly in excitement as he

realized they were stopping for the day. Rick cringed a little as Owen let out a surprised squall. Tina beat feet, and he let the dogs out and told Opus to stick close to the van. He hadn't seen an area just for dogs and most places required animals, even service animals, to be leashed. He wasn't being irresponsible, his dogs just had good training. Most of them. Sarge took off after something furry that went up the side of a tree like greased lightning. That had Opus's interest and he trotted over, followed by Ophelia who had her nose to the ground.

Rick changed Owen quickly, who had gotten over being startled by the dogs. He had what he called toxic waste disposal bags available for this purpose and tied off the offensive biohazardous material safely. He'd find a trash can and get rid of it, but if he needed to stretch, Owen, who'd been sitting all day, really needed to get out and move. He was right, he was closing the van door when Owen took off across the empty parking lot to where Tina was emerging from the bathrooms. The further south they had come, the warmer the weather. Rick was thankful for leaving the little man in jeans, but the way he picked his feet up and put them down had him grinning.

"You got him?" Rick yelled to Tina.

"I got him," she called back.

Opus abandoned the tree as Rick went to the back of the van and opened the double doors back there.

"You've been a good guy," Rick told him, and Opus chuffed in agreement and licked his lips at the sight of the big white cooler.

"You don't feed him raw meat!" Tina called. "We can't afford his meals if he suddenly turns picky on us."

Tina walked back, hand in hand with Owen, who was doing what Rick called Oomi Zoomi talk. You ignored the first half of the sentence and picked out the real words then tried to guess the meaning.

"You want me to get the charcoal going?" Tina asked, pointing to a BBQ pit that wasn't too far off from the parking area, near a pavilion and picnic table.

"Sure," he told her.

Tina let go of Owen for a second, who decided to head to the tree Sarge was still circling. She gave him half a look then grabbed the bag of charcoal, the lighter fluid, and a lighter that Rick had conveniently put in a five-gallon bucket without a lid. She loved his brain, but sometimes he took his lists and packing too seriously. However, it also made life easier, like right now.

"Owen, don't you go that far," she called after him.

He'd gotten bold and decided to go toward the next tree, but he wasn't far off. Ophelia quit sniffing all around the tree and bounded over to him, her head pushing him gently to the left. He let out a squeal, and Ophelia did it again and again until he was running in Tina's direction.

"Hi, Momma, gooolacka ooopie doopie," Owen said while laughing and holding onto a handful of Ophelia's fur.

"Don't you rip her fur out, she might get you!"

Ophelia turned her head and started licking the baby's neck and the side of his face. He let go and started wiping immediately. He stayed out of trouble and stayed close with the help of Ophelia and Sarge while she got the charcoal lit. When she turned around, Rick was carrying the smaller cooler.

"Want a beer?" Rick asked her.

"Just one," she told him.

THE DOGS AND OWEN PLAYED WHILE HIS PARENTS watched. Opus was always nearby, but between Owen and the humans he owned. His human, Rick, had brought out drinks to go with the meat sticks he grilled and the meat patties he'd made for the dogs, over Tina's objections. They were good, and his body craved more, but he knew he was full. He'd found some small rodent earlier while the cooking was going on. He'd left it for Ophelia, but she didn't want it. Sarge wasn't one hundred percent for sure what he was supposed to do with it, so Opus ate it. If he found another and killed it, the pup would know what to do.

The evil squirrel overlords were relentless in their mockery, so practicing on the smaller cousins of the prey kept him young at heart, and he was passing lore on to a new generation to ensure they kept their humans out of trouble.

"Opus, you want a beer?" Rick asked, cracking one open.

"Don't," Tina said.

"I'm not, not really," Rick told her, still holding the can down.

Opus walked up and sniffed it, then turned his head and sneezed once. Twice, three times. The liquid they were having smelled foul. He'd rather eat a half rotten cat than drink that swill.

"He doesn't want one," Tina said. "Good Opus."

Opus chuffed his agreement with her. With both of them having the foul-smelling drinks, he knew they must be planning on staying. It was a new area, and although the big green machine that gave him rides was parked out of the range of the long-tailed furry terrorists, he'd have to be vigilant. He'd have to convey the danger to his pup. Ophelia had the best nose of the trio, but Sarge might someday grow larger than Opus. He didn't mind, there were worse things in life. He made a good balance between him and his mate.

———

TINA CRINGED AT HEARING THE LOUD AIR COMPRESSOR THAT was built into the big air mattress. She knew it blew up in less than a minute, but it was the loudest thing out here. They'd had the park to themselves and watched the coals from the grill flicker and die out with the setting of the sun. Owen didn't stir from her lap, and two of the three dogs were near her. Opus, out of curiosity, was walking around the van and looking at the trees.

"They can't get us from in there," Tina called softly.

Opus made a grunting sound and continued to do whatever it was he did. Ophelia sat up and put her head on Tina's lap.

"Does that noise bug you, sweet girl?"

Ophelia looked at her and made a chuffing sound and then sniffed at Owen. She was ready to push her back just in case the dog was going to start licking him, which they did often enough thinking he needed to be groomed... but she didn't. She trotted over to see what Rick was doing.

"You know, this has been peaceful, little man," Tina said, running her fingers through Owen's locks. "We had the park to ourselves most of the evening, had dinner, a couple of drinks and we can even camp here tonight. Well, not really, the park closes at dusk which it is, but the parking lot doesn't."

Sarge got up and stretched, one leg stuck out behind him, then another. He got up on the bench across from Tina, sitting upright, looking around and then up high at the trees.

"Not you too?" Tina told him.

He let out a woof, but she couldn't tell if it was because he saw something or was just sending a challenge into the wind. She generally got his body language, but he didn't communicate the same way the other two did. Not exactly.

"The squirrels can't hurt us."

"Drop bears can," Rick called over to her as the compressor shut off.

"Drop bears are a hoax," Tina called back softly.

"Nuh uh, I saw it on YouTube."

Tina handed him Owen, and when they all walked to the van she saw half the floor space was filled with a bed and there was just enough room to set up a narrow Pack-n-Play they'd salvaged from an abandoned unit. The front seats were full of the gear they'd had in the back, and Rick had explained to her how many times he'd done this on hunting, camping, or fishing trips. She didn't mention that even though he was probably wealthy, he still pinched pennies so hard they'd scream and streak his fingers, but she didn't mind this. It was peaceful and serene.

"Bed's all made. Dogs can have their usual spots. If we crack a window, we won't get too much moisture inside and..."

"Race you," Tina said, stepping up on the tailgate.

"That's no fair," Rick told her, hands full of baby.

He handed Owen up so she could put him in the Pack-n-Play. He walked around and opened the side doors. "Come on," he called, and the three dogs bounded over. Opus was more energetic than normal after the hamburger, and Tina was pretty sure he'd caught and ate a couple of somethings. Both male dogs jumped in the middle and Opus immediately took his spot next to Owen's car seat. Ophelia hesitated and Sarge jumped in and took the spot between the seats. Ophelia instead ran around to the back of the van and hopped in.

"I don't know if there's going to be room for you back here, girl," Tina told her.

She grumbled and sat in the narrow spot between where the back door would close and the Pack-n-Play. Rick slammed the side doors, then came to the back and climbed in. The moon had risen and although it wasn't bright, there was enough for them to see with the back doors open. The black tint made the inside very dark, but if you squinted, you could still see out from inside, but not vice versa. Tina was glad because though the big air mattress was comfortable, but it put their sleeping angle about a foot under the side windows.

"She's ok," Rick said, closing the back doors, leaving them in the dark.

"You lock everything up?" Tina asked as he crawled onto his side of the bed and pushed back the sleeping bag he'd put down.

"Yes. How about we hit the bathroom in the morning and just drive through to Miami tomorrow?"

"No shower?"

"I'll find a place along the way," Rick assured her.

"Good," Tina said snuggling in, pulling the blanket over her legs.

That was when Ophelia made her move and jumped up on the bed. Tina was about to warn her off when Rick moved slightly and she crept up to about their knees and laid there, her head between them.

"This isn't going to work out if she pushes me off the bed again," Tina said.

"She's very protective of me," Rick told her.

From forward of them, Sarge let out a quiet bark.

"Don't wake the baby," Tina scolded, and Opus let out a grumble.

They settled in, and Tina found herself surprised that she was easily falling—

"YOU, *BITCH, COME OUT HERE!*" LANCE SCREAMED.

Tina backed up and hit the call button.

"Get away from me!" she shrieked.

"911, what's your emergency?" a voice said, but was so quiet she could hardly hear.

"I'm in the..."

Lance shrieked and banged on the door so hard that it deafened her.

In a blind panic she pulled out drawers. A weapon, she needed a weapon. Her right hand was full, so she tossed her phone as another blow hit the door, the jamb starting to break, the sound like an ice cube with warm liquid pouring over it, cracking. She pulled open her makeup drawer.

There!

11

RICK

Tina woke up with a start, making me come awake myself. I sat there in the darkness trying to figure out if she was going to fall back asleep from her nightmare or not. She'd curl in tighter to me until she found sleep again if that was the case. That was when Ophelia started making a low rumbling sound, her fur standing up. Owen moved in his sleep, then sat up himself.

"Doggie," I said, putting my hand on the side of the netting.

Opus let out a low warning growl. It wasn't his, 'I'm talking to you' voice; this was his 'I'm about to rip a face off' voice.

"Rick," Tina nudged me.

"I'm awake," I lied.

"There's something out there," Tina whispered.

"Out?" Owen asked, putting his hands up.

My eyes had acclimated well in the pitch black of the

van, and I could make out his form. He was on Tina's side and she reached for him, sitting up.

"I'm getting out," I whispered.

"No, I see something—"

The side door of the van opened. Opus' quiet, low growl turned into a sound I'd rarely ever heard. If a badly running chainsaw and a tyrannosaurus rex on crystal meth could blend voices, that was what erupted from his mouth as he scrambled over the car seat. I was knocked to the side as Ophelia launched herself into the middle row and all three dogs were barking and snarling.

"Oh my God," Tina shrieked, clutching Owen to her as a man's screams sounded from outside.

I don't think he understood what was going on, but in my rush to get outside, my feet got tangled in the blanket and I fell, smacking into the back door. I kicked my legs free of the blanket as Owen started crying, and I found the latch to the door in the darkness. I got out, the moon lighting things up for me to see a man curled in a fetal position as two of the dogs were whipping their heads side to side, one with an ankle, the other with an arm. I couldn't tell which, but one of the dogs was going for the beefier portion on the figure, the butt.

"*Nein*," both Tina and I chorused.

Opus and Ophelia let go immediately as if tasered, though they were still snarling.

"Sarge, off! Now!" I shouted in an angry voice, and surprisingly, he did.

I could hear Owen crying behind me, even over the sounds of the crying figure on the ground. He tried to get up, but Opus rushed in again, his head darting low. The man curled up again. Behind me a light clicked on, and I could see the shredded pants and lightly bleeding arm of a man in his late twenties, slightly underweight, with wild hair, and a wild beard.

"Sit," I commanded as Tina walked up.

She had my Beretta in her right hand, the flashlight in her left. As far as being a prepper goes, I'd just failed. I'd busted out there in my pants. That was it.

"Owen?" I asked.

"Back in the Pack-n-Play."

"Please, don't sic them on me—"

Sarge let out a snarl that had even Opus turning and looking. Tina shone the flashlight on him, and I saw a scrap of cloth hanging out of his mouth.

"What you got?" I asked.

He walked to me stiff legged, not looking away from the man, and dropped it at my feet. Then the man rolled over and it made sense. Sarge had ripped the pocket out of the ass of the guy's jeans.

"All three of you, sit and stay," I told them.

Tina gave a harsh bark of German or Hungarian and all of them went to her and sat in a line in front of her. I knew I was getting better, but she was good. She'd told me that Opus was trained to use commands in different languages than the usual police or military service dogs. It was unique to the trainers that Opus and Ophelia had come from. It cut down on somebody giving a conflicting command, one the dogs were trained to follow. They might hesitate if it came from the wrong owner, and they'd refuse if commanded to attack their owners, but it was pretty handy when she wanted them to all behave.

Sarge learned from her and from following the other two.

"They won't move until I release them," Tina told the man. "Get up slowly."

She handed me the pistol, and I held it low, but mostly pointing at the ground in his general direction.

"I'm sorry, don't sic them on me again. I promise, I'll be out of your—"

"What were you doing?" Tina asked, shining the flashlight in his face.

He squinted and held a hand up to protect his eyes.

"Looking for some food, man. I mean, ma'am."

"Homeless?" I asked him, realizing his state of dress and condition.

"Yeah, I stay in the park on the other side of the creek."

Tina shot me a look, but in the dark I was focused on him. Behind us Owen started settling down as he heard our voices. I was thankful for that at least. I know him crying in fear or anger always got my blood pumping hard, as well as getting Opus and Sarge fired up. Ophelia was the ice queen in her own way, very reserved. My red-hot anger had taken me from fight to flight and mellowed out into something else entirely. The adrenaline dump was making me shake.

"You go check on Owen," Tina said, and it made sense; even though I was the guy with the gun, she had three furry missiles ready to be launched at his near helpless form.

"Owen buddy," I said suddenly, loudly.

"Dayee," Owen gave half a sob.

I was blinded by the light clicking on earlier but could see Owen's form moving in the back side of the Pack-n-Play. I made sure my gun was on safe, then tucked it away. I pulled Owen up, careful not to bang him on the low ceiling before turning and heading back to where I could hear Tina talking to the guy who tried to break into the van.

"It's ok, we got..." My words trailed off as I saw the three dogs had taken points around the man who was now standing on his feet, a mere three feet from Tina.

"Everything ok?" I asked her nervously.

"This is my husband Rick, and that's my baby, Owen."

"Oh man, I'm sorry, I didn't realize you guys were van lifers," he said, his voice downcast.

I noticed he was rubbing at his back, but his arm was scratched up.

"So you were going to just rob a random van?" I asked him, a little bit of the anger still bubbling up inside of me.

"I was looking for food, maybe some change or something I could pawn off," he said, staring at his feet.

I looked down to see what was so interesting and realized he was wearing a pair of flip flops that appeared to be repaired with duct tape. The anger melted again.

"Listen," I told him, "you're lucky that my wife is a world class dog handler. If these three weren't so well behaved—"

I'd moved to stand next to Tina, but Opus blocked me and rumbled low.

"What's wrong, bud? You want mom to handle this?"

Opus turned and looked at me, then deliberately

turned his head to stare at the baby man then side stepped without fully turning my way to block me.

"Ahhh I see," I told him, and Opus chuffed.

Tina turned back to the man. "I'm Tina and these are our fur babies."

Ophelia daintily sneezed, and I grinned at the absurdity of this moment.

"We've got some food in the van we can set you up with for a while. I think Rick might even have a pair of shoes or boots he could part with, but what you're doing... It's not going to end well for you."

"I'm sorry," the man said, his head down, "aren't you going to call the cops?"

"Is that what you want us to do? Get you locked up for something petty so you can have three squares a day?"

"I don't want to go back to prison," he said and shivered, rubbing his arms despite the Florida heat. "It took me too long to kick the junk and stay clean."

"Then... we won't call the cops," Tina said.

"Barshy?" Owen asked, one chubby hand pointing at the man.

"What's your name?" I asked him.

"Barnes. Roy Barnes," he said.

I WAS DEAD TIRED. WE DIDN'T GO BACK TO BED BUT HAD instead got my Coleman stove out and cooked everyone food. It was the larger one I kept in the van for camping purposes. Roy marveled at how we fit things in the van, especially with three dogs that were almost 100 pounds each. He told me a bit of his story and I must say, despite being tired, I was fascinated. See, at first, I was wary of him but when I saw how completely pathetic he was, something in me broke.

Roy had been struggling with depression and anxiety his entire life. He'd enlisted in the Army at age nineteen but had failed a random drug test and had been booted out with a general discharge. His parents were so horrified by him getting bounced, that they'd enabled some tough love type action, including cutting off communications with him. He'd spiraled even deeper in depression and found himself doing stronger and stronger drugs. He'd started with pot, then moved onto meth, hashish and others. His first bust was trying to buy from an undercover cop. His second one was a raid on a drug house, where he was found passed out with a needle in his arm.

As a repeat offender, he was given more than a slap on the wrist as he'd had more than a few hits on him. I marveled as he told me all of this. What really was fascinating was how he'd been living off the land, more or less. He was thin, but not three meals away from death's door.

"What do you do for food usually?" I asked him as we were eating our second family-size packet of mountain house, split up between the three of us.

"I fish mostly, but I've got a few snares, working on a deadfall. Swamp cabbage and—"

"Swamp what?" Tina interrupted.

Owen was snoring softly in her left arm as she

cradled him and ate with her right hand. I had an idea of what he was talking about, but I'd never seen it before.

"From the Sabal Palm. You cut it right about at the heart. Kills the tree, but the inner portion tastes like cabbage and it fills your stomach." Roy answered.

"Where do you stay?" Tina asked around a mouthful of stroganoff.

"In my van," the guy admitted. "It's not often I run across any van lifers out here. I'm really sorry."

I waved that off. "Van lifers. You've mentioned that before, what is it?"

"It's... Huh, maybe you aren't. I thought you were. Basically, it's people who live out of their vans. It's technically homeless, but more like camping in a really small RV."

Tina caught my gaze and grinned. "I mean, you're all equipped for it here. If you didn't have the crib and the bench seat you could probably set you up with a small office inside there, work digitally."

Again I caught her grin and tried not to roll my eyes. She'd catch it with the rising sun, and I'd be dead meat.

"So the van people are all digital nomads?" Tina asked.

"More like... hobos than nomads. We go where the work is. At national parks like this, we can stay for free and there's often wash stations, bathrooms and, if you know what you're doing, free food."

"Except you've lately resorted to stealing..."

"My van broke down," he told me. "I've been stuck out here for a week and a half. Without a way to charge my phone the choice is walking into town in some really beat-up shoes, or take the easy way out..."

I admired his candor, but it made me wonder how much trust I should give the guy. If he could drive around, he was sort of all set, but he couldn't do much more than the initial five-mile radius of the middle of nowhere, where we were at.

"Rick is pretty handy with engines. How about when the sun comes up you show us where your camp is and we'll see what we can do."

"Are... seriously?"

"Sure," I told him, watching as Opus stared up at the trees.

12

RICK

Fixing the van was actually something I could do. Turned out, his battery had died and the voltage on his alternator was barely in the acceptable range. I got his van jumped and slipped him a couple big bills to go buy a new alternator when Tina wasn't looking. Then I gave him a box of long-term storage food and we headed out soon after 8 a.m. Owen never woke up for that but definitely did about midway through the day when we finally stopped.

"Are we there yet?" Tina asked, looking around.

"Almost," I told her.

"What are you thinking?" Tina asked me suddenly as I stopped at a gas station.

"Roy," I admitted.

"His story is a little sad."

"Actually, I was going to use him in a book," I admitted.

"What?" Tina asked me suddenly.

"Homeless, living off the land, fishing for food, harvesting wild edibles in the national forest. Hunting, trapping..."

"The kind who lived for fun before you and I..."

"Yeah," I told her. "We still do, but I just do it with more style and panache."

"Panache? Is that a word? I'm going to look that up," Tina said, pulling her phone out.

"You good back there, little man?" I asked, looking in the rearview mirror.

Tina had mounted a mirror to the back of the seat so even though Owen was facing backward, he could look to the front and see me via my mirror. It was a convoluted idea, but it worked really well.

"Hi, Dayee!" Owen said, "I out?"

"I don't know; I'm getting some gas, ask your mom."

"Out?" he asked as I stepped out of the van and shut the door.

My van was a late 90s Dodge. It got about eight to ten miles to the gallon and could pull a house off its foundation with the torque the motor produced. I kept it well maintained and babied it, but now was the part I dreaded. I slid my card in and, when it clicked off at the $100 point, I waited, then slid the card back in and finished filling it up. See, War Wagon had two tanks and I always expected that, and while driving this beast cross country was fun and comfortable, it took so long to fill it up I almost wondered if it'd be better to have driven the big RV.

"You want to grab us some Cokes and snacks while I change Owen?"

"You want to grab pops and snacks and I can do the diaper for once?" I asked her back.

"I love you," Tina said sweetly and then bounded out of the van just as the pump kicked off.

I stretched, then opened the side door of the van. Ophelia got me first, then Sarge. Both had been waiting at the side door, ready to slobber on me.

"Oh man," I said, wiping my face.

Ophelia looked especially pleased with herself. For a while, she had jealously guarded me from everyone, including Opus and her own pup, but she was relaxing a bit.

"Move over, I have to change a stinky. Sit on my seat!"

Both dogs didn't have to be asked twice. Opus looked over the car seat at me and yawned. I got Owen out of the harness, then pulled the diaper bag to me. I laid him down on the bench where Ophelia usually sat when we all rode together and did my husbandly duty, hoping it would win me some points for later on when we were at the hotel and dog-less. I was considering getting a two bedroom or adjoining rooms or...

"Uggg, that smells," Tina said, surprising me as I was finishing getting him buttoned back up.

"Yeah, you want the extra safe toxic waste disposal bags?" I asked her.

"Naw, just going to toss it here," she said, putting it in the trash bin next to the fueling station. "I've got candy bars, beef jerky, some meat sticks and a bunch of pops to put in the cooler."

"I'll take some jerky and a Coke Zero," I told her.

She snickered, having already guessed what I was

going to get. I put Owen back in his seat and although he wasn't too happy about it, I sat in the van with him while Tina let the big dogs out to go to the bathroom. She put the mandatory leashes on them, and I watched as people stopped to stare. Opus was by far the largest of the three and was getting the most attention. We were used to that.

"Oppy, Offee, Barge!" Owen exclaimed, pointing point the side window.

"Opus, Ophelia, and Sarge," I agreed, then looked to where he was pointing.

Two of the three dogs were standing near a tree looking up. It was the boys. I had to grin. If Opus ever caught another squirrel I'd be surprised. That had to have been a one in a million shot, because he and his son were staring intently into a palm tree near the grassed in area. I finished the buckles and five-point harness long before Tina had finished, so I closed up the van and got it started to let the air run. I marveled at how just a day and a half previously I had thought winter was upon us and here in sunny, stormy Florida, it was in the seventies.

"We're going to go do a Mommy and doggy pickup," I told my son through the rearview mirror.

"Mama!"

Tina must have heard the motor fire up and looked over, but Ophelia was pulling her lead so she could use the restroom in a spot not occupied by the other dogs. I pulled next to them and when she was ready, Tina walked over and opened the side door, letting the fuzz butts inside after taking off the leashes.

"Go ahead and get up front," Tina told the dogs.

I saw Opus take his spot right behind me, but both

Sarge and Ophelia scrambled for Tina's seat as she slammed the door closed and took the bench seat next to Owen.

"I promised them," she told me by way of explanation. "Hey, I heard a tropical storm might be coming through here in a few days or so."

"Good thing we're going on a seven day cruise," I shot back. "Did they say if they expected it to turn into a hurricane?" I asked, remembering how Irma had devastated the coasts of Florida.

"They didn't say anything like that, but they did say to expect rain and wind."

"We're from Michigan, we're used to a little rain and wind," I told her, but secretly felt slightly uneasy.

THE HOTEL WAS NICE. NOT IN THE WAY A HOWARD JOHNSON in Michigan is nice, this was almost mind-blowing nice the way my first luxurious hotel in Utah was nice. Because I was a penny pincher at heart, I'd avoided places like this, but not this time. Since we'd made better time than I had thought, we had the dilemma of figuring out what to do with the dogs. It wasn't like when Annette was at the hospital with Bud and we'd slept in the van. Here, we risked cooking them in the dark colored vehicle without the air running. I was discussing the dilemma with Tina when the check-in clerk, Gloria, heard our problems.

"We do have pet-friendly suites available, I can check and see if there are any available?" Gloria asked us.

"That would actually be amazing," Tina said, wrapping one arm around me with a hot, sweaty, smelly, cranky Owen on her arm.

"Ok... Let me see," she said, tapping on her keyboard.

Brown hair, Hispanic heritage somewhere in there, but her accent wasn't what I was expecting. It sounded like she was from Kentucky somewhere. I took in her features the way I'd started to, memorizing her so I could later use her in a story somewhere. Maybe as a foil or a bad guy in this new post-apocalyptic book I'm writing.

"What kind of dog?" she asked without looking up.

"German Shepherds," Tina answered.

She looked up, "How many?"

"Three," I answered.

"Bree, Dayee! Dayee, bree!"

"Yes, Daddy said three," Tina said, bouncing him.

"Three German Shepherds..."

"Two are service animals, the third is in training. Actually, Opus is nearing retirement," I told her, "Vacation for all of us."

"Ok, let me see... Just a moment..."

"Sure," I said, feeling like the size and number of dogs was suddenly going to be a problem.

It was something we'd run into before, especially since we'd gotten Ophelia and she'd had a litter of pups. They were family to us and we knew what to expect from them. It just seemed that there was a stigma with large dogs; people were afraid. They only had to worry if they tried to hurt one of us... other than that, there wasn't a problem. A moment later, a man came out from behind the doors with Gloria and approached us. I saw his name was Clint, and my heart dropped a bit when I read 'Manager'.

"Hi, I'm Clint. Usually we allow two dogs per guest. In the case of service dogs, we count them as another family member. I'm just curious if I can meet this trio before you guys head upstairs?"

"Sure," Tina said, giving him the 10,000 watt smile.

"It's not usually company policy to ask... but I was a handler in the Marines. It's been a long time and... I have a soft spot for Shepherds."

I took in his features. Mid-forties, clean shaven. A scar on one side of his cheek, and underneath the collar of his button-up shirt I could make out the colors of an artful tattoo. I looked at his wrists and sure enough, one of the sleeves was pushed up slightly where what looked like the tail of a dragon stuck out. His hair was close cropped, but I could tell he had some ink under the hairline as well. Covered. I don't know why, but I immediately liked him.

"Sure," I took Owen. "You, sir, are getting a clean butt and a shower," I told the squirming toddler.

"Down, me down?" he asked.

"If I do, you better not run off. I'll have to get Opus to fetch you," I told him, putting him down.

"Oppy no get," Owen said and then held onto my pants leg, realizing how many people were in line behind us and got the sudden case of the shies.

"Oh wow," Clint said, looking over my shoulder.

Tina had my set of keys in her hand, her other hand held three leashes loose. I realized with dawning horror they weren't leashed. A fancy hotel like this would never... The automatic door opened and Tina walked exactly two steps behind them, murmuring something then giving a command. They all sat as if at attention.

"Oh man," Clint said, coming around the counter. "You work with them much?" he asked her.

"Opus here is a certified therapy dog, Ophelia's got the papers, but she's about four now. The guy who looks like his paws are as big as his head is Sarge, he's got a bit of growing to do."

Clint walked over and I heard Gloria murmur something under her breath in an uneasy voice. I watched, smiling and feeling that Owen hadn't let go. Clint knelt in front of the three of them and took them in one by one. Then he stood up and looked over Opus who was on the far left. He walked around half way then got in front of him and knelt again.

"You're a soldier," Clint told him.

Opus chuffed and put a paw down in front of his other one then pulled it back, a motion I hadn't seen in a while.

Clint muttered something that resembled the commands that Tina used and I hadn't learned yet. Opus went tense, his head cocked to the side. A low growl emitted from his throat.

"Not a good idea," Tina told him, "his working commands are a combination of German and Hungarian, and not the usual formats either. Give him the wrong ones, he might think you're trying to trick him."

Clint hadn't moved his ground, but instead offered up his hand, "Sorry, bud, I was just asking," he finished in English.

"Is he…?" Gloria asked me.

"He's fine," I told her. "Opus is vocal; that wasn't really a growl, that was him telling your boss no."

"What did he ask him?" she whispered back.

"Nothing much," Tina said. "Fetch is what I think the direct translation was."

"Yup," Clint said, standing up sheepishly, "He sits a little off set. Bad hip?"

"Old gunshot wound," Tina answered before I could. "He's also eight."

"Not just a soldier, but an old vet. You, sir, are very well mannered and the rest of you are well behaved. I don't think we'll have a problem."

Ophelia let out a whine, and Clint put his hand out in front of her to sniff. She leaned in, and that was when Sarge's patience ran out. He broke his stay command and walked over, his tail wagging so hard it was almost making his whole butt sway. Tina let out a frustrated sigh and gave me a grin.

"Owen's Barge!" Owen let go of my leg and toddled over and put his arms around Sarge.

Clint watched, suddenly nervous as Owen hung his weight off Sarge's shoulders and neck. He stood there and turned his head to start licking my son. He started shrieking in laughter making people around us look over at the commotion. Owen fell on his diapered butt in giggles, and Sarge put a paw on his chest and continued giving him a bath.

"They usually—"

"There's nothing usual about our dogs," I told him. "They've literally saved our lives." I grinned, not facing him but watching my two big boys give Owen a spit bath.

The rest of the people around us had noticed. They seemed alarmed at first, but saw how the dogs were doting on him and his laughter was shrill but full throated and genuine.

"You guys have a nice day! If you want, later on tonight at the beach I've got my Coco girl. We play frisbee—"

Opus barked once, his entire body moving to the rhythm of his tail.

"That sounds like an enthusiastic yes to me," Clint told us.

Ophelia looked at Tina, who murmured something, and the other two dogs who had been sitting still got up and pushed their noses in Clint's hands. He gave them some pets, and I scooped Owen up. He suddenly was trying to swing a leg over Sarge's back. Sarge, for the most part, was just sitting there taking it, but he gave me the look. The 'help me, I don't want to be a dufus and hurt the baby by accident' look.

"Ride?" Owen asked, pointing down.

"No, we don't ride the dogs," I told him.

"Your key, and the Wi-Fi password is written on the side."

"Perfect," I told her.

OWEN ATE PART OF A HAMBURGER PATTY AND ALL OF THE fries I'd ordered up from room service, drank a bottle, and crashed hard. It was almost 8:30pm, so it wasn't horribly early. I had been trying to work for the last twenty minutes, but my lap was occupied by Ophelia. She'd been sharing me for so long, that with Tina, Opus, and Sarge out playing in the sand, she didn't want me to move off the couch. The front of her body and her head was in my lap, her feet hanging off the side. For a moment I thought she'd fallen asleep and tried to scoot, but she woke up and wiggled further onto my lap.

"I want to check on your mom," I told her.

She grumbled a bit, so I scratched her ears until her grumbles turned into groans.

"I have to work also," I told her.

She scooted even further. I reached over and snagged my laptop bag and pulled it close. I'd packed my Surface Pro as well as my regular laptop. The Surface Pro was an amazing device though. It had all the features of a laptop, but it was the size of a large tablet. It was an amazing machine, if a little hot when in use heavily. It featured a solid state hard drive and more RAM than a writer would ever need, but it had my Dragon files and transcriptions on it as soon as I synced it up.

I booted it and turned the TV on. The news was talking about the tropical depression. Tina had told me tropical storm. I felt a little less worried than I had before. Then I checked the time for the third or fourth time in the last ten minutes and started working.

13

OPUS

His shoulder was sore, but in a good way. He'd gotten to take his human and his pup out on the sand for a good chase and run. They had been without their usual exercise for a few days, and it made him grumpy and sore. The air smelled different here than it did back at the house. He could smell something salty and there was almost a fishy smell in the air, like the fishing hole where his human Rick had the big moving house.

All of his humans were sleeping. He wasn't though, he'd slept too much in the van and was now in that half awake state but couldn't quite sleep. His mate and pup were sprawled out on the couch. On padded feet, he pushed the bedroom door open. It didn't creak like the ones back home did. He walked quietly over and sniffed the sleeping human child. He smelled like soap, his breath stank of French fries and milk, and he snored softly. Then he crept over to see his human, Rick, had fallen asleep with one arm hanging off the bed. He put his nose on the arm, then licked it.

Rick murmured something and pulled it back and put his arm under the covers. His original human he had adopted was sort of half using Rick as a pillow in the middle of the bed. She barely made any noise, and he cocked his head sideways. Tina moved her head and looked at him.

"It's ok," she whispered.

Opus put his head at the foot of the bed.

"You can come up if you want," she whispered, patting the bed with her free hand.

He walked around to the other side of the bed and sniffed. Beds in rooms like these often smelled like cleaning supplies, other people, and food. This one was no different, but he wasn't looking for any of that. He was merely smelling things to see if something triggered a memory of danger. His nose was not as good as his mate's, but he knew trouble when he smelled it. He'd always remember that sickly black smell coming off the man who'd hurt Rick and was wary of it. He'd only run across it once since then, but the human had wisely stayed away with a quiet warning.

"You need to sleep," Tina called softly as Opus padded out.

He made a circuit of the entire suite, especially the kitchen, where he debated raiding the bin that humans put their waste food containers in. He could smell a French fry and knew the small human hadn't eaten the bun the meat came on. He sighed. He had a reputation to uphold. One last place to check since the main door was secured. Opus padded silently to the sliding glass door and put his nose against it. They were high up, he didn't know how high, but heights made him dizzy. There was a nice soft rug right here, and the air vents were blowing cool air. He turned a circle and sat down.

Ophelia heard him somehow and she got up from the couch, one leg stretching, then another. She walked over to Opus who watched her with one eye. She sniffed the rug, then turned in a circle to find the best spot and settled in, her head resting on his back legs. Opus let out a contented sigh.

Tina had planned on beating Rick awake, but she found him up at 4:30am, furiously typing away. She did the zombie walk over to the kitchenette where she could smell a pot brewing. Owen was still out cold in the Pack-n-Play.

"Why you up so early?" Rick asked suddenly.

"Was going to try to get up before you and get some breakfast ordered up and take the dogs out," Tina mumbled.

Rick slid her over a steaming mug of coffee. She looked at it, then at him, then back at the coffee maker.

"Second pot?" she asked.

"Guilty," Rick told her. "This new storyline is really coming together."

"I was wondering. Owen went down hard last night and when I came back in, it looked like Ophelia was competing for attention with your tablet."

"She was, she's a jealous girl sometimes, kind of like my wife."

"I am so not jealous," Tina said.

"No, not really," Rick told her. "Besides, who'd make you breakfast and have coffee ready for you if I didn't love you so much?"

"If Opus had opposable thumbs..."

The coffee wasn't the cheap stuff, it was a rich Columbian blend that had been sugared and creamed the exact way she liked it.

"You heard me waking up?" she asked.

"I knew sooner or later you'd be up. Without me to keep you warm and you having the world's smallest bladder and..."

"Thank you. Coffee first, bladder second; I'll get the dogs. You need to keep writing all the words."

Rick nodded and gave her bottom a squeeze. Tina almost spilled the coffee, but managed not to scald the both of them. She was about to say something snarky to him, but decided not to.

"Opus," Tina said, walking over to the patio door.

Opus woke up at her voice and looked up at her.

"Going to be time to go outside soon. Want to wake up everyone but the baby while I get ready?"

Opus chuffed, then got up slowly, stretching. That woke up Ophelia and when they turned to look, Sarge was laying on his side, his eyes open and his tongue hanging out of his mouth.

"You bunch of fakers. Rick must have woken you up already."

Sarge chuffed.

14

RICK

Tina and Owen took the dogs to drop them off at the boarders. I stayed behind and worked. It had been a long time since I'd been on fire the way I had been on this book. I was used to writing fast, but this was coming out twice the speed I was used to. The words flew off the keyboard and onto the screen in a blur. I had some bumps when I was trying to get back into the flow after editing some old transcribed words, but I'd already fixed and edited that and smoothed things together. My process compared to other writers probably sounded odd to some, but it was what worked for me.

A knock at the door interrupted my train of thought. Had I ordered food? I couldn't remember. My vision swam back into focus instead of narrowed into the world I'd been writing. The knock came again. I got up and went to the door and opened it.

"Annette?" I asked, confused, seeing her standing there with a bag in her hand.

"I caught an earlier flight, now you guys don't have to pick me up."

"How did you get here from the airport?" I asked her.

She held up her phone proudly. "Uber," she said with a smile.

"I didn't think you liked using your credit card online or with your phone?" I asked grabbing her bag and opening the door wide.

She stepped in and looked around, smiling. "I decided to surprise you and this nice lady on the plane told me about Uber. So when we landed she helped me set everything up. Took five minutes. Then I just told them where I wanted to go and poof, here I am!"

"Poof!" I agreed, smiling back.

For a moment, I thought her smile was because she was finally free of Sarge, but I immediately beat that thought into submission. She was on an adventure, and she had done something she'd probably not done alone her entire life. She'd crossed the country, ordered a cab with her smart phone, and put one hell of a surprise on me.

"Lord, you had to have grabbed a red-eye or something?" I asked, closing the door behind her.

"I flew out at 6:40 this morning," she said. "Where's my munchkin and fur babies?"

"Uh huh, not excited to see me, just excited to see—"

"Oh shush, I'm just kidding. Tina take them out for a walk?"

"We're boarding them at a kennel nearby for the cruise. She took Owen with her so I could get some work finished up."

"Am I interrupting?"

"No," I told her truthfully. "I should have quit and ordered lunch a while back," I said, looking at my watch. "You hungry?"

"Famished!"

"Let's head down to the restaurant and grab some food then."

"Shouldn't we wait for Tina?" Annette asked.

I slapped my forehead. "Yeah, let me text her."

The door made a clicking sound and then Tina was walking through, a diaper bag over one shoulder, Owen on the other arm.

"Grammy!" Owen cried.

Tina gasped and put him down. He ran to her and almost tackled her to the couch. She laughed and sat down, picking him up. He curled into her and rested his head against her shoulder.

"Oggys go bye, bye," Owen told her seriously.

"Yes, they can't all come on the ship with us, can they?"

"When did you get here?" Tina asked, her face a mask of confusion.

"Just now; I Uber'd!" Annette said in a gush.

"We were thinking about lunch, what do you think?" I asked Tina.

"You forgot to eat again?" she scolded.

"Don't worry, I'll have an extra beer to make up for missing the calories." I grinned.

"I think I'll have one too. Owen, you want to go to eat?"

"Eat? Deliciousness?" he asked.

"Yes, but no more French fries," I told him.

"French Fries!" he exclaimed, making the ladies roll their eyes at me.

I should haven't said it out loud.

WITH OUR EVENING SUDDENLY FREE OF HAVING TO PICK UP Annette, Tina and I found ourselves alone and walking on the beach. Annette had offered to watch the little man. He was almost out from a full day of fun in the sand and sun. In the morning we'd all get on the cruise ship, but for tonight, Tina and I were alone.

"You had the dream last night, didn't you?" Tina asked me.

Shit.

"Yeah," I admitted.

"How often now?" she asked.

"Almost never, but when it hits, I can't go back to sleep. How about you?"

"I had it the night Roy tried to break into the van," she admitted to me.

I knew there had been something, but I wasn't sure if I'd been dreaming or if it was part of her waking me up. I shook that memory off and took her hand. We'd been walking on the beach in our bare feet, letting the surf coat our legs as it came and went.

"I miss Bud," I told her suddenly. "I never thought we'd lose him. He's just so—"

"Ornery," Tina finished.

"Exactly. I almost feel like this trip so soon after his funeral is somehow... Improper?"

"Maybe you feel that way, but I don't," Tina told me. "I think we're doing exactly what he would have wanted us and Annette to do."

"Celebrate life?" I asked her.

"You do get it sometimes, even if you pretend you don't."

"How late you want to walk the beach tonight?" I asked her.

"The concierge said half a mile down there is a Tiki Bar. Let's get some drinks and maybe dance in the sand a little bit."

"I'd like that."

The wind changed, and instead of the gentle, warm wind that had been coming off the water, this was colder air. It brought with it the smell of ozone.

"We better hurry," I told her, "I think it's about to rain."

"We could jog there," Tina said. "It's been forever since you've had a proper workout."

I dropped her hand and took off. I heard Tina let out a frustrated yell, and I could hear her splashing behind me. I was bigger and much heavier, but Tina's advantage was she was smaller, lighter, and had been building her endurance on running for a long time. Years and years. Barefoot in the wet sand and through the surf, I could feel my legs start to burn, but she hadn't overtaken me yet. I looked down the beach and saw the building she must have been talking about. I could make out torches with the backdrop of electric lights.

"Almost..." Tina panted from behind me.

I put on a burst of speed. I heard Tina say or yell something behind me, but her words were lost in the sound of the surf, wind, and my pounding heartbeat. People saw us running and turned to watch, some grinning when they realized I was being chased, or raced. My breathing was beginning to become ragged. I'd been jogging with her for a few years now, but I was not a sprinter. I could jog long distances, but not at the rate I was going. I put everything I had into it and got just a little more speed out of it. For the first time ever, I was going to win, I was—

Tina went shooting past me, laughing so hard that I thought she'd fall. I pushed harder, but I was running flat out. Another thirty seconds and I caught up to her as we stopped, panting. I walked into the surf a bit and let the water wash away the sand that had caked up around my legs from the mad dash while I caught my breath.

"Not sure I've ever seen you run like that," Tina said, barely out of breath.

"Not used to being chased," I told her.

"I wasn't chasing you, I could have passed you a while back."

"Yeah right," I said, feeling like I might puke.

I should have avoided the two beers and heavy lunch.

"Let's go get some drinks," she said, pulling me by the hand.

STINGRAYS TIKI BAR WAS EVERY BIT A TOURISTY TRAP IN

the world, but somehow I loved it. I'm an introvert by nature, preferring to be alone or with a very small core group of people, but this place was packed without setting off any sort of anxiety. We were sitting at one of the tables near the bar with a small fire ring in the middle. No doubt running off propane or natural gas, but as the sun had gone down, the night had chilled and people had started heading to tables like ours.

"You ok?" Tina asked me.

"Oh yeah, little tipsy," I admitted.

I'd been drinking a concoction called a rum runner. It was a Florida Keys special. At first, I thought it was going to be a frufru drink, but it was killing me. My third one was probably one too many, but the fourth was what I was working on. I was feeling good and we could always walk to the street and call an Uber.

"What do they put in these?" I asked Tina who had been the one to suggest it to me.

"Two kinds of rum, some juice, some other liquor and then a shot of 151 down the straw."

I was going to be feeling real pain in the morning. I pushed my drink back and stretched. We'd danced a couple dances as a steel drum band played by the fire, no real moves, no rhythm, just a slow dance. My race earlier had made my legs sore so we hadn't done many. We'd instead done what we always seemed to do. Talk some, snipe at each other. Talk about life. Tina wanted us to go to Arizona next summer to see her parents with Owen. I'd told her the desert still held bad memories for me. We talked about why, books, writing, how her eBay business and the mini-storage was the perfect business for her.

"It's potent," I told her.

"Then drink up and we'll walk back to the hotel," she said.

The way the table was laid out, it could easily seat twelve to fifteen people. The benches were round like the table, so her words weren't lost on the younger ladies sitting to her side who started giggling and whispering. I got up, a little tipsy, and took a tiny sip of my drink and put it down. I dug out a twenty and put it under the glass.

"Ready," I told her.

The world swayed a bit as the alcohol and exhaustion hit me all at once. We made it just past the torch light of the tiki bar when I felt something shove me from behind. I fell hard on my face and was rolling over when I heard Tina let out a surprised shout. I got to my feet to see a figure sprawled on the ground and Tina standing with her hands up in what almost looked like a boxing stance, her whole body swaying. The figure was getting on his hands and knees when she kicked. She hit him in the side and he screamed out in agony, rolling on his back.

"Sucker tried to steal my purse," she said. "Get your phone, call the cops."

"I wouldn't do that if I were you," another voice came out of the darkness.

It was another man, and I couldn't see him well in the dark, but I could see the reflection of something shiny in his hand. A knife or a gun?

"You ok?" I heard a couple people yell from the bar, probably thinking I'd fallen down.

In fact, I'd been shoved.

"Help!" Tina screamed.

The man figure in the dark looked left and right, then reached down and pulled the writhing man to his feet as Tina and I both backed away. I'd already felt for my right hip and sworn as I realized I'd locked the gun in the van so I wouldn't have to do it before the cruise ship tomorrow morning.

A couple of lights lit the night and the two men took off running. The girls who had been sitting next to us came out of the dark. I saw their faces for a moment before the bright light of their phones' flashlights blinded me. I held my hand over my eyes.

"You ok? I heard a yell and you called help?"

I looked at Tina who winked at me and took half a step forward. "He fell and I couldn't get him up at first," she lied.

"Oh, well, are you ok?" the younger one asked.

"I think so," I said, brushing sand off me and trying not to puke.

I hadn't been hit hard when I was knocked over. I'd probably been bum rushed as the guy tried to run between Tina and I to grab her purse. Instead of going to plan, I'd stumbled and fell and Tina had unleashed her Kung-Fu. Actually, I think it's Krav Maga, but I don't ask because it would go back to why she needs self-defense classes and a protection dog. Some things are still too raw to say out loud.

"Ok, we can call you a cab if you like," one of the girls said, shaking her phone and making the light cut off.

"I think we'll be ok," Tina said. "Thanks for checking on us."

I waved at the ladies who were returning to the party

and looked over at Tina. There was just enough moonlight for me to see her clearly.

"Why?" I asked her.

"I don't want to spend all night with the cops and potentially not get on the ship on time. It leaves bright and squirrelly!"

"You know, you kicked that guy's ass pretty good," I told her. "I'm totally impressed."

"Better than the day you jumped over my counter and Superman punched a bad guy?"

"That was damned impressive, I don't care who you are," I told her. "But the kid was right, maybe we need a cab. I'm pretty wasted, and I should have seen that coming."

"I've been drinking cranberry and spritzers all night and I didn't see it coming. Besides, I think they ran off toward the road."

"The beach it is," I said.

"The beach," she agreed, hooking her arm through mine.

"So will you beat up anybody else who tries to hurt me when I'm drunk?" I asked her.

"Just give me a target, asses will be kicked."

"Good," I told her. "I'm drinking a couple bottles of water when we get back. I don't think I ate enough, and those three and a half drinks shouldn't have looped me like that—

15

TINA

Rick was almost a zombie by the time they walked back to their room. Annette took one look at him and moved off the couch so Tina could get him to sit down.

"What's wrong? Drunk?" she asked.

"I don't think so, he had a few but not enough for it to have made him this bad," she said pulling his shoes off. "I've seen him drink more once or twice and he was nowhere near this bad."

"Drugged?" Annette asked.

Tina opened her mouth to say something then closed it again. He had complained that the drinks had hit him hard with the last one. Was it possible? Had they counted on Rick's reflexes on being slowed to rob them both? Were those girls in on it, or somebody at the bar? Her mind swirled with the possibilities. Still, she wasn't sure. She pulled Rick's phone out of his pocket and looked up the number of the bar, then got her phone out.

"What are you doing, dear?" Annette asked.

"I'm going to call the bar, see what they think," she said and hit send with her free hand and tossed Rick's phone on the couch next to him.

RICK WOKE UP TO SEE TINA, ANNETTE, AND OWEN GETTING everything packed up.

"How are you feeling?" Tina asked.

Rick moaned, "Not good, what happened?"

Annette shared a look with Tina, and his wife came over and sat down with him.

"Rick, that last drink you had last night was spiked."

"What drink?" Rick asked.

"The... They said this might happen. Listen, you remember anything from last night?"

"Walking on the beach with you, then racing you. Wait, is everything ok—" A note of panic crept into his voice.

"No, everything's fine," Annette assured him.

"Then what...?"

"What do you remember?" Tina asked again.

"Running in the surf, racing you?"

"Yes, go on," Tina urged.

"Ordering drinks and then... Did I fall and hit my head?" Rick sat up, his hands going to his head and wincing.

"Somebody spiked your last drink. You were feeling tipsy so you didn't finish it. Somebody tried to steal my purse last night... Don't worry, we were both fine, I scared him off."

"What?" Rick asked, rubbing his hand over his face.

"Anyway, the two ladies who'd been sitting with us drinking Sprites... they checked on us. I got you back here and you passed out, basically. I called the bar to ask them if they knew anything, but they didn't. About an hour ago, the Miami PD called. Apparently one of the gals finished your drink off. Too young to buy their own, I guess? Anyway, her friend called 911 in a panic. When the cops got involved they tracked down the bartender who put them in touch with me. They say somebody tried to slip you a roofie."

"Was it the guys who tried to steal your purse?" Rick asked, his voice pained.

"I think so. The police are tracking that down, but they said you would sleep it off easily. Now that you're up, if you hurry, we can still get on the cruise ship!"

Rick got up slowly, his legs wobbled and made his way into the bathroom. Owen tried to follow, but Annette scooped him up and deposited him in Tina's arms.

"Dayee.... Ewwwwwwwwwwww...." Owen started to say as the sounds of retching came from the bathroom.

"Maybe we won't be on time after all," Annette said.

"We won't miss it," Tina said with a smile. "We have an hour and a half until we have to be there, and we're ten minutes away. The Waze app on my phone says traffic is light, and I can practically see the dock from here."

Louder retching came from the bathroom, making Tina's confident smile falter a minute. "Maybe I should get this guy in the shower. Owen, you stay out of trouble."

"Ubble!" Owen echoed.

Tina was ready for a mess, but found Rick upright and wiping his mouth out.

"Sorry, I made myself puke. I feel hung over and wanted to purge anything left in there," Rick said sheepishly. "I should be good to go after a shower."

"I wasn't sure how bad off you were going to be," Tina admitted.

"Well, as long as you were looking out for me, I wasn't worried."

"Wait, is that a compliment?" Tina asked, smiling at him.

"You take that crazy karate stuff. You're tougher than you let on."

Tina smiled, not caring to tell him the entire story. She didn't want to worry him, and she'd rather he not remember her going savagely feral when she'd kicked the guy in the kidney area. She wasn't proud of that, but she had been pissed at their evening being ruined. That, and the man knocking Rick down and almost tearing her off her feet.

"I am. You get your bad self ready—"

"Dayee, hi!" Owen said, squeezing in the bathroom between Tina's knees.

"Hey, buddy. You look all spiffy."

"Iffy!" Owen agreed and then began to tear at his clothing.

"No showers with Daddy. Come on, I'll find you some Bubble Guppies or Oomie Zoomies."

"Ooom uppies!"

"I think he wants both," Rick said as he scooped up Owen and handed him to Tina.

"I wan Dayeeeee!"

"Not this time. Daddy has to wash off the yuck, yuck!"

"Teenky?" Owen asked, a hand grabbing his mom's chin and pulling her face to meet his.

"Definitely stinky."

Rick mumbled a curse under his breath and took his shirt off. "Can you run me some clothes in? I feel like crap, but I think some hot coffee and a steaming hot shower will do wonders for me."

"I can do that and don't strip till I get out of here, we still have a guest."

"Oops! Sorry," he said as Tina edged out of the door and pulled it closed behind her.

"I wan Dayee!" Owen repeated.

"Let's watch cartoons," Tina redirected.

Annette had heard it all, and the show was already on TV. When Owen was put down, he crawled up on the couch next to her. Tina got Rick's lists out from his laptop case and sat down. She knew everything that was in the bags they were taking on the trip. They'd gone through everything before they had left and those bags hadn't been touched. Other things, like Rick's gun, would have to go into the safe bolted underneath his seat, but she suspected it already was there. Same thing with any knives. She went through the banned items list he had printed off and compared it to the list of things he'd packed.

"What are you looking for, dear?" Annette asked.

"I'm just double checking—"

The TV made a loud noise and then the Emergency Broadcast System came on. Tina turned back to Annette, having heard that test at least once a day. That's when she realized that it wasn't a test. They were talking about a potential tropical storm. It was expected to hit northern Florida, but there was a wind advisory going into effect later today as a precaution.

"I asked the cruise line about this," Annette said, "back before Rick got the ticket... I was worried because it was hurricane season. They just take the big boats out to sea where they can ride it out if it gets really bad, but this? This isn't nothing."

Thunder crashed outside, making them all wince.

"I hope..." Tina began.

"Me too," Annette told her.

"My Grammy," Owen said, pulling Annette's arm around him.

"You trying to make Mommy jealous?"

Owen giggled.

16

RICK

I let Tina drive the van. Despite not liking to, she was an expert. I did tease her that I'd have to put a phonebook under her butt so she could see over the steering wheel, which didn't amuse her much, but it did me. I sat in the back seat with Owen. He was babbling up a storm. He was trying to figure out how to say more words and, when Tina missed a turn she said something that, for the first time, Owen parroted exactly. I busted up laughing.

"That's not going to help," Tina said, turning.

"Maybe he just said truck?" I offered, still grinning and seeing the baby's face light up for getting a reaction out of me.

"No truck. Fu—"

"Let's not say that, buddy," I told him, putting a finger over his mouth.

"Thank you," Annette said. "Though if Bud was here, he'd probably say Owen is ready for his first cigar and whiskey."

Tina giggled and turned again. "Hey, I didn't miss it by much. This takes me to their parking lot too!"

Tina managed not to ding, bump, or dent anything and backed into a spot near the back gate. I was going to ask her to, but like always, she was reading my mind.

The unpacking went quick, we each had a large rolling bag, and all of Owen's extra stuff not in the diaper bag was packed in my suitcase. Tina's, of course, was full. Packed to the brim. Had to sit on it to get it to zip shut, and then Opus had to help so she could move to zip it. I still had some room left over, a fact I didn't mention to her. I wanted to bring some souvenirs back. I scooped up the little man, dragged my backpack and felt that there was something missing. I turned back to the van, hiking Owen further up on my hip.

"What are you looking for?" Annette asked, her own roller bag in hand.

"I don't know—"

"He's looking for the dogs," Tina said.

I looked at her, realizing she was absolutely correct. I nodded and then closed the side door. Tina ran around checking the locks before dropping the keys in my pocket.

"Everybody got their passports?" I asked.

Annette groaned, "Is he always this anal?"

"Anal?" I asked her.

"You mean a list-making worry wart?" Tina said, patting her back pocket. "Of course he is. We checked this before we sat down."

My head was still fuzzy and sore from last night. I just nodded and tried to keep up when Annette and Tina set the pace. It was brutal. It was like the intermittent sun was jabbing daggers into my eyeballs, and my stomach was a roiling mess. I hid it well, but what scared me was how much of the previous night I didn't remember. I didn't remember getting bowled over, and I didn't remember Tina running them off. I didn't remember a clear night turning into a stormy day.

"Dayee, iiiip!"

"Ship?" I asked him.

"Iiip!" he said, pointing.

Sure enough, it was a word he had learned on his own from somewhere. It was *HUGE*!

"That sight gets an old lady's heart a racing!" Annette said.

"Let's check in before it starts raining," I said, looking up, feeling that cool wind blowing through again.

BY THE TIME WE GOT CHECKED IN AND OUR BAGS TO OUR room and unpacked, I was ready to get some food and sit down. A portable crib had been delivered and Owen was sitting in it, playing with a couple of the big plastic Chuck trucks Tina had got for him. He was laying on his side, his movements slowing down. He'd thrown an absolute fit and had wanted to start running as soon as we got onboard, but that wasn't happening. Not yet.

"You hungry?" Tina asked.

"Yeah, but little man looks like he's going to go down."

"Want me to go grab some food and bring you some

back?" she asked, probably knowing how wiped out I still felt.

"That sounds good. You going to check on our neighbor and see if she wants to go?"

"I think I will. Who knows, maybe get her out and mingling with others?"

"It's too soon to match make!" I shot back.

"I wasn't going to, but she might want to meet people her own age so she doesn't feel like she has to hang out with us the entire time, if she doesn't want to. She and Bud lived up north mostly alone for a while. I know he was a bit of an introvert like me, but I don't think she is."

"Gotcha," I said, then she grinned as I yawned.

"You and baby cakes hold down the fort. There will be food back when you both are done with your nap!"

"Our?" I looked over and the little guy was out cold, a car still in his right hand.

"Yes. You're still not feeling good, I can tell."

"Busted. Maybe a few rum runners would fix that?" I said, to get another grin and an eye roll.

I WOKE UP TO A QUIET ROOM. OWEN WAS STILL ASLEEP, BUT Annette and Tina were nowhere in sight. I was used to having a dog or a toddler or Tina usually on the bed or couch next to me. I got up to test my stomach out and found it had settled during my nap. I used the restroom and checked out our room. It was spacious, but it definitely was on par with the nice hotel room we'd had. There was a TV mounted on the wall, a large queen-sized bed, a table and chairs for two, a small fridge and enough dresser space to unpack our clothes and a large closet to hide our suitcases in.

I walked to the window and looked out. I could see the deck in front of us, the railing, and could see that we were underway. The clouds were dark and I could see the deck was wet, but it didn't look like it was raining right now. I went and found my room key on the table next to my laptop bag and pocketed it. That was when I saw the note.

There's sandwiches in the fridge. You were out cold, so I changed Owen, gave him a bottle, and put him back down. He must have not been done napping because he was out cold really soon after that. Annette and I were invited by some ladies she met to play shuffleboard. I can hardly contain my excitement. Come up on deck and save me when you and Owen are ready! First few rum runners on me!

I snorted and went to the fridge. It looked like she'd brought me back a couple club sandwiches. I took one out and unwrapped it as I walked back to the table. I'd work for a little bit and then bring the baby man with me. I dug into the food and booted my laptop. I'd heard that the internet here was almost $.75 a minute unless you bought a big enough package. I wasn't really planning on needing the internet, but it'd be nice to at least back up my work once a day.

I was thinking all of that and scarfing down the first quarter of my sandwich when I heard Owen's breathing change. As a parent now, I'd learned the sound of the kiddo breathing when he was awake, and when he was sleeping. When he had a cold or if he was excited. Right now, he was waking up. I closed my laptop and finished my sandwich off.

"Momma," he said softly.

"I'm in here with you right now, buddy," I told him, standing up.

His view of me had been blocked by the bed, but when he heard and saw me, he sat up, rubbing his eyes.

"Eat?" he asked, seeing me chewing.

"Sure," I said, picking him up.

He was warm and soft in my arms as I sat him on the end of the bed. I used to worry about him falling off, but he'd mastered the art of getting on and off our bed at home that was slightly larger than this one. We had to upgrade when Tina was pregnant because Opus and Ophelia wouldn't stay on the floor, and Tina had turned into a raging bed hog. Worse than her usual using me as a body pillow.

"Down," Owen said.

I'd been carrying him toward the fridge, but put him down instead. "Eat?" he asked again.

"I'll get you something. Let me see what else Mom put in the fridge here. We'll get you squared away and then go find her.

"Oppy go bye, bye."

"Opus did go bye, bye. He's at a playground for dogs," I said, stretching the truth a bit.

I opened the fridge and was looking at the sandwich wondering if I could get him to eat parts of it when I saw a fruit cup she had brought back from somewhere. It wasn't a prepackaged cup, but cut up chunks of fruit in a clear plastic cup. She must have realized that he'd wake up hungry. Here I was, the first one interested in prepping and my wife constantly was two or three steps ahead of me. Must. Up. My. Game.

"Come eat this," I said, finding a package of plasticware on the wire shelf of the fridge.

"Oooooooh kaaaaay" Owen said, running my way when he saw what I was holding up.

He hit my leg and squeezed. "Rute!"

"Fruit, looks like apples, pear, banana and maybe some pineapple."

He giggled and I tried to move my leg, but he wrapped his legs around my ankle and his arms just over my knee. I walked, dragging him and making him squeal in joy, to the table. I put the food down and then moved my computers to the bed. Then I plopped him in the opposite chair of where I had been sitting earlier. He was still mastering tableware, but he managed to make a minor mess, something I cleaned up easily with a wash cloth from the bathroom. I changed his butt before venturing out to find my wife.

"Oh he's a cutie," some young ladies, probably late teens, early twenties, told me as I left my room.

Already, daily clothing was being abandoned for bathing suits. These two had probably checked into their rooms long enough to do a quick change, but I felt out of sorts and hardly noticed.

"Thanks, Owen, you want to say hi?"

Owen turned his head into my shoulder and then waved at himself. The girls giggled and gave him a wave goodbye. I turned and looked around and saw the stairwell to go up a level where I heard raucous laughter from what sounded like shenanigans. Venturing out without a diaper bag made me feel dangerous and out of control, but I would feel like a total dork if I had a Mickey Mouse diaper bag over my shoulder. I hadn't thought to pack my backpack—

"Oh there you are!" Tina said, coming down the stairs I was coming up.

"Hi. Thanks for the food, hit the spot, for both of us," I told her.

"Here," she said, holding her arms out.

Owen had already been leaning her way so I handed him over. He started trying to get her glasses, but she switched hips, telling him to knock it off, giggling like a girl at his tomfoolery.

"Where's Annette?" I asked.

"She met a couple ladies her age. They've already started calling themselves the widowers club wives."

"Oh lord..."

"Oh don't worry. They made a pact to have fun and avoid single guys," Tina told me. "Let's get off the stairs. I was just coming down to check on you guys, or we could go back up?"

"Let's go up," I told her. "I haven't seen much here other than our room while I snoozed for an hour or so."

"Ah hour or so?" Tina asked, grinning, and turned, leaving me watching her climb the stairs.

I followed. "My phone won't have signal they said, so I turned it off."

"It's almost supper time," Tina said, waiting for me at the top of the stairs.

"Oh wow. Hope I didn't ruin dinner by scarfing down that sandwich?"

"No, probably not. I guess they serve dinner late. Annette said she'd watch Owen for us after supper if you wanted to go out and..."

"Have a date with my wife?" I asked her, an eyebrow raised.

"Something like that," she said with a mischievous grin, "or something more."

I liked the sound of that, I liked it a lot.

17

RICK

I lay in bed, waiting on Tina to come back. I could still smell her on the bedspread and I felt amazing. Dinner, drinks, dancing and the hangover from earlier was gone. We'd come back to the room for some alone time, but Annette said she wouldn't knock unless The Little Tyrant woke up and wanted one of us. She'd given Tina a spare keycard so she could let herself in as well as a salacious wink and a hip bump.

Man I felt good.

The doorknob jiggled, and I got up. Annette had had a crib sent to her room as well and for what little extra they charged for it, I didn't mind the cost. I figured Tina had her hands full of baby man, so I opened the door wearing nothing but my boxers. I pulled it open and—

"Oh no, wrong room!" one of the young ladies from earlier said, then hiccupped as I tried to close the door.

"That has to be it," another said pushing against the door I was trying to close.

"You got the wrong room," I told them.

"You got a guy in our room?" the drunker of the two asked. "When did you pick him up? Looks kinda nerdy. He better have a—"

"Ladies," I said loudly, "you've got the wrong room."

"Yes, ladies," Tina said from behind them.

I opened the door at the sound of her voice and saw the dynamic duo turn, surprise on their faces.

"You took home the guy with a baby?" What the hell, one of the ladies punched the other on the arm "No single dads!"

"Ladies..." I said as they started arguing.

"Excuse me," Tina said, ducking between them and in the doorway.

Owen was starting to wake up, and I wanted the noise to end. It had to be two am or later. I started pulling the door closed when the less drunk one started for the door again. I slammed it before she could reach it and hit the deadbolt. She started pounding on it and yelling.

"She's going to wake up the baby," I fumed.

"Too late," she said as Owen sat up in his crib and started crying.

The pounding on the door continued. Our house phone rang and Tina answered it.

"Yes... no, wrong room. They're really drunk... I guess they got the full Monty. No, Rick answered the door... well, yeah. No, no, he had his boxers on. Yeah, if they don't stop in a sec I will, or maybe I'll send Rick back out there."

I could barely make out her side of the conversation as I looked out the peephole. The less drunk one was the one doing the pounding while the other held up her keycard and was squinting at it under the light.

"You're on baby duty," Tina told me, storming the door and trying to push me aside.

"Hold on, you don't want to do that; let's just call security or let me."

"They already got a good show from you," she said, pausing to look me up and down.

Her hair was tousled from the alone time and she was savagely beautiful in that moment. Being the alpha male I am, seeing her in an utter state of pissed off, I got the hell out of the way and picked up the baby. He quieted, but was still sniffing as Tina threw open the door, letting it stay open behind her.

"You ladies got the wrong room," she said loudly to the lady who almost knocked Tina in the head not realizing the door had opened.

"Oh hey, it's you. What are you doing in our room?"

"This is our room, which room you got, hon?" Tina asked her, though I could hear the annoyance in her voice.

"302," she said immediately.

"That's your problem then," Tina said, the anger draining and she relaxed a bit. "We're in 320, see, right here?"

The girl looked at the door number stupidly, then turned back to her friend who was still trying to read the felt tip marker on the card's sleeve.

"Says 302," the drunk one slurred.

It always amazed me that people could get so blind piss drunk and not die. That was how it must have looked to Tina when I was roofied, but these two were getting annoying.

"I just want to lay down," the drunker one said, pushing her friend out of the way to be stopped by Tina, arms on her hips in the doorway to the room.

"This isn't your room, go find your room."

She tried to dodge under Tina's arms, but she just moved and her head hit Tina's stomach. She pushed her back. The drunk let out an exasperated sound and tried to bum rush her way through like a drunk version of red rover. Tina didn't flinch and the lady bounced back again. She stood up and reached for Tina's hair. That was when I saw my wife do something so brutal I'd never forget it.

She punched the gal in her bikinied boob, then once in the stomach. She started to slump, but Tina pushed her back. Less drunk friend just gaped in surprise.

"You should be going now," I called over Tina's shoulder while the one on the ground retched and dry heaved. "I'm calling security," I said, putting Owen in the chair by the table.

Tina slammed the door and shot the deadbolt. She turned to Owen and walked over, scooping him up. He made a happy baby sound and laid his head on her shoulder.

"I'll talk to them. Shoot, I hope I don't get in trouble," Tina said, suddenly nervous.

"She tried pushing her way past you, then tried to knock you over. Looked like self-defense to me."

"Yeah, I just... she wasn't going to stop."

I looked at the card that was set by the phone and

found security. I handed her the handset and dialed it. She swayed with Owen in her arms while she waited.

"Yes, Tina from 302. We just had an incident with a guest. Uh huh, oh no, nobody's hurt; well, not really. Oh no, don't need a doc, but probably going to need cleanup. They were drunk and tried pushing their way into our room. They... yeah, the one gal said they were in 302. Not the first time? Really? I had to punch the one girl in the... uh huh. No, I didn't hurt her, just knocked the drunk out of her I think. Yeah, I think they are. Pretty dumb if you ask me, even without being drunk. Uh huh. Ok, thanks," she hung up the phone.

"Want me to check if they are still there?" I asked her.

"You can if you want. Apparently Annette and a couple other rooms have already called security. They were up on the fourth floor earlier trying to find their room."

"That's sad," I told her.

"Well, lets not let the commotion ruin our good night."

"You going to call Annette back?" I asked her.

"Let's see if we can get Owen to sleep. Move his crib out from the middle of the bedroom area and give us some privacy?"

"Again?" I asked her in mock surprise.

She shook her hand where she'd made a fist. "As much as I feel bad punching a drunk, that felt good."

I remembered the drunk in Wyoming. He'd almost gotten much worse, but I remembered the feeling after he'd left. It was a savage joy that you felt in the center of your chest. I'd let Tina take her frustrations out on me. It was the least I could do.

I WAS ALMOST DRIFTING TO SLEEP WHEN I HEARD WHAT sounded like an alarm somewhere faint. Then the PA system. Tina was half laying on me, one leg hooked over my waist. I listened and with the small nightlight in the room I could see the fire alarm light we had. It wasn't going off and the harder I listened, the more I was convinced that I was half dreaming. I was exhausted mentally and physically.

"SO I HEAR YOU THREE HAD SOME EXCITEMENT?" ANNETTE asked at the breakfast table.

"Not much," I told her.

"It wasn't really anything," Tina told her, though this morning she had admitted she felt horrible for punching that lady.

"Well, as long as you two were able to get some good sleep in."

"I'm not sure Tina had sleep—" Tina kicked me under the table, making my leg jerk up, rattling glasses and silverware of everyone within five feet, which was quite a few.

"Owwwww," I said, rubbing my shin under the table.

"Dayee owwwie. Momma kiss?" Owen asked Tina just as she was taking a drink of water.

She sprayed it back into her plate and started coughing. Annette was sitting next to me, but she started laughing out loud, holding onto her side. I let it go on a moment, but Tina was still coughing. I got up and walked around the table behind her and pounded her on the back a couple times. She held a hand up, and I snuck a sausage link off her plate and put it on Owen's. His sudden interest in what was vexing his mom was gone as he started devouring Elkridge Farms meat of the gods.

"Oh uh... Hi," a voice said from across the table.

Both Tina and I looked up. She coughed a couple more times, and then wiped her mouth with a napkin.

"Sorry, wrong pipe," Tina explained.

That was when I did a double take. The ladies had their clothes on and weren't in bikinis. The gals from last night.

"Listen," the lady who got boob punched started, "I want to apologize for last night, I'm really sorry."

"You make it to your room ok?" Tina asked instead.

"We did, security helped us, then the ship's doctor threatened to pump my stomach if I ever drank that much again. Lord, I barely remember last night. I'm really sorry, I didn't mean to upset you, your baby, and your husband."

"I'm sorry for the wrong room mix up," the other one said. "I didn't want to wear my glasses. They look stupid and I have this eye thing and can't wear my contacts right now."

"I—" I started but was interrupted.

"Listen, I've been young and had my fun times like you ladies are doing here"—they nodded— "but, this could have turned out real ugly. What if you would've got some abnormal rando who pulled you both in his room and did God knows what?" Tina asked.

They looked at each other uneasily.

"Being a lady, you have to be careful about getting that drunk and losing control like you two did last night. Things could have gone much worse."

"Worse than me getting punched in the boob?" the one lady asked, rubbing her chest unconsciously.

"Tied up, locked in a closet, being hurt over and over and over. You two were so drunk you probably wouldn't have remembered most of it, and even if you did, who would believe you. This society takes things like how we dress and how we act when weighing motivations. They might even think you were wanting it and when you sobered up—"

"Let's not get too graphic," I said, putting a hand on Tina's shoulder.

Their eyes were as big as saucers.

"I'm sorry. I..."

"Beans!" Owen exclaimed loudly.

"What does beans mean?" Annette said, probably hoping to ease the tension.

Owen made a face and I moved away from him toward my side of the table. "Listen, I'm not upset about last night. I'm glad you two are ok. Just take my wife's advice and avoid drinking that much and getting that drunk."

"Well, at least you weren't some abnormal rando," the other girl said, grinning, then turned to Tina. "He works out, doesn't he?"

Tina turned red, but I couldn't tell if she was merely furious or something else.

"We all do."

The young lady who asked whispered something to her friend who looked at me, then Tina. Then she waved to Owen who ducked and tried to hide his face. Then he peeked and waved backward.

"Beans!" Owen said straightening up.

"Ok, listen, I'm really sorry. No hard feelings?"

"I'll think about it," Tina said, "I'm not pressing charges if that's what you were wondering."

"Wait, you could have pressed charges?" the woman asked.

"Yup," Tina answered.

Annette paused the bite of food that was going to her mouth to look at Tina, then bit into her omelet.

"Ok, well, we'll be going. Hope to uh... not get lost and confused again. I won't drink like that, I promise... and I'm really sorry." The last of that was said as her friend was pulling her backward.

We all watched them walking away, our group and everyone else who was within earshot. A couple people shot me quizzical looks and I shrugged my shoulders, noncommittal. Tina went back to her plate and looked down, then up at me, then to Owen who'd just taken another ham-fisted bite of sausage.

"How'd you get that?" she asked him.

"Beans!" Owen repeated again, and that's when I realized what he was telling us, he stank!

I heard the PA click on.

May I have your attention please. We are asking all guests to return to your rooms for an emergency drill. We need the corridors open for firefighters and first responders. Please stop what you're doing and return to your rooms in a calm and orderly manner.

Tina looked at me and sighed. I grabbed my plate while standing and shoveled the last two bites of my eggs and sausage into my mouth, wiped my mouth, and held my hand out for Annette. She swatted it away, scowling. Tina grabbed Owen out of his highchair seat and we headed to the staircase that led us down to our rooms. We weren't the only ones, the walkways were filling up with people heading back down.

It wasn't long until everyone started doing the right side going one way, left side the other. It became less chaotic, though it still took us ten minutes to walk back to our rooms.

"Want to come in?" Tina asked Annette.

"I don't mind if I do. How else am I going to find out what you left out of last night?" she said with a wicked grin.

"Like what?" I asked her.

"You punched a lady in the boob?" Annette said, sitting on the edge of the bed.

The cleaning crew hadn't been in yet, and I straightened the bed up as much as I could. It was obvious to me that there had been a wrestling match or two last night, but Annette didn't say anything. I wondered why she sat there instead of the table, but as soon as Tina sat Owen down, she started undoing his clothes.

"You figured out beans?" I asked her.

"Smelled it. Are you teaching my grandson that awful rhyme?" she asked me pointedly.

Tina gave me a look and I nodded back. She'd called Owen her grandson. It filled me with happiness.

"I might have said it a time or—"

"Forty," Tina finished.

"Wait, you knew what beans meant?"

"I uh… yeah, but I didn't know if he was done," I said suddenly seeing the trap for what it was.

"That's ok, I've changed a lifetime's worth of dirty diapers. This one is yours."

I sighed.

WE DIDN'T GET THE ALL CLEAR TO COME OUT OF OUR rooms right away like I thought we would. I could see up and down the aisleways that they were clear except for staff scurrying, but I smelled something. Burnt plastic? I didn't see any smoke, but a ship this size was literally a floating city. I turned on the TV after trying general information and getting a busy signal. Then the PA clicked on.

We regret to inform you that we've had a fire in the mechanical and food service portion of the boat in the lower decks. The fire has been put out and cleanup operations are going as we speak, but we have to return to port.

We find it prudent to also note that our weather associates have been updated that Tropical Storm Leo has turned into a hurricane. So far its track has changed slightly south and is looking to head to South Carolina. Normally we'd stay at sea, but with damaged systems, if the storm changes direction we might be in a worse situation. We can return to port by this time in the morning, two days ahead of the storm.

Guests will be refunded the cost of the cruise if they do not wish to rebook at a later date. We hope to have you back with us soon. One last thing, it is now safe to return to your usual activities as the all clear will be sounded momentarily.

I heard the ringing or dinging sound over the PA which probably signified the all clear, and I turned to Annette and Tina.

"Well crapola," Tina said.

"Ola!" Owen repeated.

"So much for a drill earlier, eh?" Tina asked.

"You got that right. Probably didn't want to panic everybody," I told her.

"My flight doesn't leave for a week," Annette said, biting her lip.

"Rick can fix that, easily. With his computer," Tina assured her.

"You aren't upset that you're missing most of the vacation?" I asked her surprised.

"Oh yeah, but I mean... there was a fire. If it's bad enough to turn around a cruise like this and offer refunds... It must have been bad."

"I didn't see any smoke," I mused, "but I did think I smelled something."

"Electrical fire?" Tina offered.

"Quite possible," Annette told her with a nod.

"Crap, that means we have to pack. No late nights for us, buddy," I told Owen.

"Well, maybe I should too," Annette said, standing up.

"Meet up for lunch?" Tina asked.

"If you don't need me to watch Owen, I might sneak upstairs to gossip with the girls and grab some tequila," she said, dropping a wink.

We both waved as she left, Owen finally getting his hand turned the right way.

18

RICK & OPUS

Getting off the boat was much faster than boarding. I'd spent some time and money last night and got an internet bundle. I hadn't done much writing, but I had been able to get Annette's plane tickets switched. Since I didn't know how bad traffic and getting out of the parking lot was going to be, we went from the boat straight to the airport. I was expecting the traffic to be bad, and it was. We weren't the only cruise ship to unload at port today, though I was willing to bet we were the only ones who had to end the trip early. I'd gotten her flight for 1:40PM and with an hour getting off, we made it out of the parking lot close to noon.

"Plenty of time," Annette said.

"You're supposed to be there three hours early," I told her.

"You worry too much. It isn't a big airport like Atlanta. I can be through check-in and security faster than grass through a goose that's had laxatives."

I crossed my eyes in frustration. I hated being late. Even with everything going good, my mental plans had been thrown off, I didn't want to—

"You're coming down from being in the crush of all those people getting off the boat. Relax," Tina said, rubbing my arm.

"Lax!" Owen shouted and started humming the '*One Two I Love You*' song.

I kept the radio off. I was irritated. The trip was cut short, we had to return to port. We were undecided if we were rebooking or taking the refund. We had to get Annette to the airport so she didn't miss her flight, then we'd go back and get the dogs... and then...

OPUS WAGGED HIS TAIL, PUTTING HIS NOSE IN THE HAND OF the human he was forced to babysit while his regular humans were gone. As far as humans go, this lady wasn't bad. She smelled like rabbit, which confused him at first, but he knew humans sometimes cohabitate with them for whatever reason. He personally loved to eat them, but to each his own.

She had the leashes in her hands and had Ophelia and Sarge already hooked up. She tried clipping on his, and he stepped sideways. He didn't need a rope to drag her to the play yard. There were lots of trees, a big fence to inspect, and he suspected that the vile horde of ninja squirrel assassins were out there waiting. He'd be ready.

"I have to put this on you, buddy. I know you don't need it," she said kindly and pet him with her free hand.

Opus stopped and considered that. Did she need to pretend to drag him out there? Preposterous, but he saw how some humans were afraid of his canine family, especially all three of them together. He held still as she leaned in and clipped his leash to his collar. He hated it, but Ophelia and Sarge weren't complaining much. He knew they must be onto this charade. To show he was a good sport, he rubbed his head against her leg, then sniffed her ankle where the rabbit smell was the strongest.

He didn't like being away from his humans and although there was a communications gap, he understood he had to be here until they came back for him. It worried him, but this was going on the third light and dark cycle. He wondered how much longer someone else would have to take care of his people while he watched over the human who smelled like rabbit.

Opus had mostly watched as Ophelia and Sarge returned the ball to the human. She liked to throw it, so he felt obliged to bring it to her a time or two. Feeling worn out, he sat down and watched as his mate and son played. The day would have been perfect if his humans were—

A scent hit his nostrils, and he let out a sharp bark. Both Ophelia and Sarge stopped as if zapped, then took off at a dead run for Opus who sat by the back door.

"What's gotten into—" The human's words were cut

off when another human he babysat walked out with... his family?

Opus barked excitedly, throwing away the usual calm exterior he tried to wear like armor. He jumped up happily, making sure not to scare the tiny human or his human, Tina. Rick laughed and pushed him back to four legs, so he threw his weight into the human's leg and pet the human with his whole body. He hadn't realized how much anxiety he'd been holding onto... Sarge and Ophelia were there a moment later, but Sarge's jump for joy almost knocked Tina and the tiny human over. Opus growled and nipped at his shoulder, startling Sarge and making him back off. Opus sat and then wagged his tail and chuffed.

Ophelia was more sedate. She sniffed everyone down, licking their clothing and hands. Opus could smell the salt in their hair and clothes. From that big blue pond he couldn't see across? That smelled worse, but it had the smell of salt also. He'd have to ponder that. Sarge walked over and put his muzzle under Opus' and pushed up.

Opus grumbled back good naturedly. Apology accepted.

"They always like this?" the aid asked.

"We've never been away from them," Tina admitted. "Not overnight."

"For a second, the big guy startled me. He's so good natured..."

"He was warning his son to not be so excited as to knock over Tina," the human Rick said.

"That looked—"

"He doesn't have a mean bone in his body, do you, Opus?"

Opus walked to the human he'd been babysitting and rolled over onto her feet, kicking his legs in the air. This accomplished two things. Well, three. He was showing her he was only playful, not mean. Secondly, he was able to rub the rabbit smell on his fur a bit. He loved the smell the way the human Rick loved bacon. Third... He forgot what the third thing was.

"WHY IS TRAFFIC SUDDENLY SO BAD?" TINA ASKED AS THE wipers were going like crazy, barely keeping up with the rain despite the sunlight.

"I don't know," I told her.

Tina pulled out her phone for the first time. We'd decided to go back to the hotel we had stayed at before because they had been so accommodating with the dogs, then head out in the morning.

"Oh crap," she said as I pulled into the hotel parking lot after what seemed like an eternity.

"What?" I asked her.

"After I got through all the messenger alerts, Twitter and eBay stuff, I checked the news. The hurricane has changed course."

Something cold and shaped like a cannonball seemed to drop into my stomach.

"Where exactly is it coming and when?" I asked her.

"All it says is that it's tracking more southerly than they expected."

"How much more southerly?" I asked her.

"Its track looks a lot like Irma's did a couple years back."

I cursed quietly. Opus put his head on my lap, and I scratched his ears.

"I'm going to head in and get us a room," I told her.

"It's going to take me a minute to get little man and the furry guys unbuckled anyway. This way the van doesn't heat up and fry—"

"It's like we're married and on the same wavelength," I said, leaning over and kissing her briefly.

Ophelia whined back on the bench seat next to Owen, who had his hand in her fur. I grinned at the jealousy she was displaying. Then again, she didn't like storms, and the nonstop rain didn't have any thunder and lightening. Yet.

"Nice," Owen said into his mirror, petting her roughly.

"Yes, you're being nice to Ophelia," as I got out and headed into the hotel.

The lobby was full of people with their bags, lined up everywhere at the counters. The mood in the room was ugly, and the front desk people were apparently all hands on deck. I wiped the water off my arms and face as I tried to jockey my way close to the desk.

"Excuse me," I asked a red faced guy walking my direction, out the door, "what's going on?"

He almost didn't stop but saw me in total confusion and must have taken pity on me.

"Hotel is closing for the hurricane evacuation," he said.

"Evacuation?" I asked him, confused; Tina had said nothing about an evacuation.

"It hasn't been called yet, but after Irma, the owners of this chain don't want to take a chance. They've asked guests to leave. At least they're trying to give us vouchers for the next time.

"Oh man, that sucks. Sorry to hear it. So the evacuation hasn't been called?"

"No, it's something the governor mentioned on the radio and these pansies are shutting the hotel down until after the hurricane has passed. If it even hits here."

"Yeah," I told him, "I'd love to have a job as a weatherman. Get your work wrong half the time and you get a pay raise."

"You got it. I'm heading to a resort a mile up the beach. Rumor was they still had openings. If they do call an evacuation though, I'm out."

"Make sure you fill up on gas before the crunch happens," I told him, "and thanks for the info."

"No problem, good luck." He gave me a mock salute which I returned. When I got outside, I saw Tina stretching, then opening the side door to let the two and four legged critters out.

"Hold up," I told her, jogging over.

"What's up?" she asked as Sarge tried to get out.

She blocked him with her legs and told him to sit, which he did.

"I guess the governor mentioned something about maybe having to call an evacuation. The hotel is shutting down until things pass."

This time it was Tina who cursed. "I didn't see

anything about an evacuation," she told me, pulling her phone out of her pocket.

"Checking on things?" I asked her.

"Hello?" she said into her phone. "Yeah. Good! Oh, you're almost on your flight? Final boarding?"

I realized she was talking to Annette. Luckily I'd rebooked her ticket while we were still on the boat, before things got crazy. I knew how fast plane tickets, gasoline, and other things went when the panic hit. I was starting to feel a little bit of it myself, but the logical side of me had already considered something like this happening and I was going to avoid panic. I got in the van and waited for her to finish her conversation.

"Things are going to go crazy," I told Opus who'd pushed his way into the middle.

Opus chuffed and put his paws on the console so he could watch Tina. I got my phone out and asked Google for a list of hotels near me.

"Me!" Owen yelled.

"Yes you," I said and saw on the map just up the road there were miles of hotels if we wanted to stop instead of bugging out.

The one thing I didn't have in my van was extra fuel. It did hold a stupid amount of gasoline, but the mileage on it was horrible. I remembered horror stories of fuel shortages from the last hurricane and how people got stranded. It would take an entire tank of gas to get out of south Florida and into Georgia or Alabama. I needed to hedge my bets.

"She's on the plane and safe. What do you think? I

know we wanted to maybe hang out a day to wait and see if traffic gets better, but I was wondering..."

"Momma!" Owen called.

"Owen!" she cooed back.

"I'm not sure if we should stay or go. We're kind of at the tip of the state. It hits anywhere near South Florida, we're stuck."

"How much gas do we have?" Tina asked.

"That was going to be my next thing. You mind if we hit up a hardware store, then the gas station before we figure out what we want to do?"

"I don't mind. Wow, look at the panic setting in."

I nodded grimly as angry people poured out of the hotel in twos and threes. It actually slowed me down from pulling out of my parking spot for nearly two minutes as people loaded. Once I was on the road, I kept my eyes peeled.

"Over there," Tina told me, pointing.

I'd already seen it, but I nodded anyway. Owen was singing some song about dinosaurs to Ophelia. He was trying to stroke her fur, but he pulled as much as he petted. She was patient and would have moved before getting annoyed.

"I'll just be a second," I told Tina.

As soon as I opened the door, Ophelia hopped off the seat and pushed past Opus and hopped out.

"You can't come in," I told her.

She sneezed. With a sigh, I closed my door to see Tina and Opus through the window, one of them smiling, the other giggling. The rain was cold, but contrast that with the wind blowing hot, muggy air, and it wasn't horrible. I remembered reading that it rained quite a bit in Florida. Was this normal, or the front of the front of the hurricane?

"Let's see if this hardware store is dog friendly. Just walk right next to me, I don't have your leash."

She leaned her head against my leg, rubbing her ear into my pocket until I pet her. She wasn't as vocal as Opus, but she still got her point across via body language, and what she was putting off as we both walked into the hardware store was more than a little apprehension.

"That's a beautiful dog—"

The clerk behind the checkout register's words cut off as if in a choke. He was mid-thirties, and looked like a local, the sun having tanned his already bronze skin. His accent sounded Hispanic. Cuban heritage? Ophelia stayed beside me as I walked over to him.

"Don't worry about her, she's the nice one," I told him by way of explanation.

Ophelia chuffed softly but obediently stayed right at my side.

"I... Sorry, you just look familiar," the man said when he found his tongue again.

"I get that a lot. Do you have any gas cans?" I asked him.

"Sure, aisle eight," he said, pointing.

I walked down that way, my hand at my side brushing against Ophelia's fur. Right away I found the cans. I bypassed the plastic ones and looked at the larger five-gallon metal cans.

"Too bad you can't help me carry these," I told her,

then grabbed three of them, the fourth barely held on by a pinky finger.

I walked up front and the clerk saw me coming and put down the cell phone he'd been speaking into. He gave me a smile.

"Find everything you're looking for?"

"Yeah. Just getting ready in case the hurricane hits and everyone panics and there's no gas."

"Yes, sounds like a good idea," he said, ringing me up.

I was digging in my wallet when he asked, "You have a lot to fill and some gas stations are already running short as people panic buy. You should stop into Joe's Towing up the street a few miles. He's got his own fuel farm and sells at the rate he buys it."

"Really?" I asked, curious, but wondering what his angle was. "Maybe I'll check him out."

"If you want," he said. "You and your girls have a nice day." He looked down at Ophelia, who remained silent.

Was it a relative of his he was drumming more business up for? The other thing that bugged me was although I did have a familiar face, and that was because of the kidnapping a couple years back more so than my writing... but he was starting to look familiar also. I got my change and thanked him. Ophelia stuck to my side like glue, so I wasn't surprised when I opened the door, she barked at Opus till he got out of my seat. She jumped in and, as he tried to get in his spot in the middle, she used her shoulder to push him back.

He looked at his spot next to Owen and sighed and got up. Sarge, of course, wanted to lick my face off, so I gave him some loving too and took the sausage bites out of the side pocket of the van and started handing them out so I could get some room.

"Need the keys to open the back," I told Tina.

"Owen has a new word. Truck a saurus."

"That isn't a word," I said, grinning.

I unlocked the back, then loaded the fuel cans in. I could always crack the back window... was this even necessary? The wind died down for a moment and I realized that the rain had stopped and the sun was out, though shielded by wispy clouds.

"Not only is it a word," Tina said getting in, "the radio lady said that they've got a new estimated track for the hurricane. I think we should bugout."

She actually said those words. God I loved that woman, even if she made sense and was telling me bad news.

"Alright," I told her, "let's do that as soon as we fill the gas cans."

"It'll get us out a day and a half ahead of when they say it's going to hit," Tina said, and her voice quavered a little bit.

"Is it going to be bad?" I asked, meaning the hurricane.

She nodded.

"If we take I-75, it heads to the western side of the state before going north. We might avoid some traffic if we take the roads less traveled, but I'm worried about running out of fuel," I told her firing up the van.

"Let's get it filled and I'll use the Waze app and see where the traffic is worst."

19

RICK

I never used the Waze app much. For as much as my life revolved around computers and software and the internet to conduct business, I didn't overly complicate things. If the road looked busy, it was busy. Tina, on the other hand, started telling me where the gas stations were going to be, and that there was going to be a huge traffic snarl on 75 going north northwest. To make matters worse, the gas stations we were passing were full of cars lining up on the side of the road to even pull in.

"You know what?" I said aloud, "Look for a place called Joe's Towing."

"What's there?" Tina asked.

"Hopefully gas. Guy at the hardware store said he's got a fuel farm and usually sells it for what it costs him in situations like this."

I passed another full up gas station when Owen erupted into tears in the back.

"Probably gassy," Tina said.

If you've ever driven with a fussy toddler, you know how nerve shattering it is. Tina reached for her seatbelt when I saw the sign.

"There it is," I said, putting on my left turn blinker and getting into the turning lane.

"He's probably got a bubble that needs to get out," Tina said. "I'll take care of that while you figure out what we're doing."

"Sounds good to me," I said, wincing as Owen wailed louder.

Opus made a whining sound, and I could see in the rearview as he put his snout in front of the baby and I lost sight of him. Owen yelled, but not quite as loudly, then stopped and giggled.

"Go," Tina said.

I looked forward and saw the way to turn was clear. I had gotten semi-distracted. I turned in, electing to pull up in the front. It was a steel building with tall privacy fencing around what had to be the impound lot. I could see the roof of what was probably a garage or covered parking for their tow trucks. I parked, then got out, not surprised when Ophelia jumped on my seat and then bounded down to sit next to me, her tongue hanging out. Opus made a disgusted sound. I closed the door to see Tina braving the middle of the van, pushing Sarge back.

Poor dude probably felt left out, but I doubted people would look kindly on a guy walking in with one big dog, let alone two. Plus, he was still a bit of a doofus, smart, but goofy. I opened the door, making a buzzer go off somewhere in the back of the building. There was a plain desk with a corded phone sitting there, a dog eared yellow legal pad on one side, and an overflowing ashtray on the other. A bathroom sat off to the side, the door half open. I'd seen gas station bathrooms in better shape than that and for once was glad I didn't have to go.

The entire joint smelled like rancid sweat and grease with a heavy layer of cigarette smoke. I heard a door open and close somewhere behind the door behind the desk. Probably to the back of this building. It opened and an older guy came in wearing blue coveralls with 'Joe' monogrammed on the pocket.

"Help you?" he asked, his accent straight out of New Jersey.

"I was at the hardware store a few miles down the road, and they told me I might be able to buy gas here?"

"Oh yeah. Not all the time, but I have some to spare right now. You getting out of dodge before this hurricane business hits?"

"Trying to. All the gas stations are full, and I've got a one ton van... Hard to pull it in and out," I said lamely, even though I could drive that thing anywhere.

I was going for the sympathy, that and a fair price on fuel.

"How much you need?" he asked me.

"I've got four five-gallon cans, and I'd like to top off my van before hitting the highway. Probably thirty-five gallons?"

"Oh that's no problem. Now my gas isn't cut with ethanol, so it's a little more pricey than gas station garbage."

"How much?" I asked him.

"I paid $3.45 a gallon for it," he said, scratching his

forehead with a grease-stained hand, "with delivery and stuff, I figure I can give it to you for about that. Say $3.50 a gallon?"

That sounded like highway robbery to me, but I did know that pure gasoline without ethanol was pricier and it wasn't like he was gouging me. For peace of mind?

"Sounds good to me," I told him, doing some mental math.

I pulled out $125 from my wallet and dropped it on the counter. "Keep the change."

"You want a receipt?" he asked me.

"No, sir."

"Ok, we're all good, I'll open the gate and let Javier do the fueling with you. Just pull your vehicle in the gate and go straight back to the pole barn. You'll see the big red tank. I'm in the middle of a transmission rebuild, and it's pissing me off."

I grinned and tipped an imaginary hat. He gave me a wave, and Ophelia and I headed out. There was the same shuffle of the dogs as I got in.

"He let out some air and has been playing with his puppies," Tina told me happily as Ophelia got in her spot.

"That's good. You figure out a way out of Florida?" I asked her.

"Still looking," she said, "How much was the gas?"

"I gave him $125 for about thirty-five gallons."

She scrunched up her face. "A little over $3.50 per gallon?"

"I know, but he said this is the stuff without ethanol

so he pays more for it. I think it'll probably last longer if we don't need to use it all at once."

"Wow, gas hasn't been that expensive in a while. At least it's the good stuff," she told me as Owen busted up into giggles.

I put the van in reverse and lined up with the gate that had started opening a crack. Owen erupted into tears again, his vocal chords really amazing. I winced, and Opus got down from his spot and headed to the back of the van.

"Oh, buddy, maybe you need a bottle and a burp huh?"

I concentrated and, when the gate was open, I pulled in. The inside of the lot was asphalt for the most part. There were a couple spots that had boats and an old camper at the back corner. The office had an open air garage built off the back, and I could easily see the pole barn. It wasn't large like I was expecting, but the fuel farm to the right of it was easy to see. I drove to the back. I saw somebody wave from within the barn.

"Be right back," I told everyone. "Ophelia, you stay."

She whined a bit, but stayed. I had left the back unlocked, so I left the van running, the air blasting. I opened the back of the van and pulled the four cans out and started taking the caps off.

"Poor buddy," I said to Owen, who Tina was working to get out of his harness.

"Help you with something?" a guy in blue coveralls with 'Javier' printed on the pocket asked.

"I bought some fuel from Joe," I told him.

"Si. Bring your cans over, he just called me on the radio."

The guy was giving me the once over, but I realized I'd been doing the same. Memorizing details, making a mental character card for him should I ever need a tow truck driver/mechanic in a book. Heck, he could be in my post-apocalyptic book I was writing. Tow truck driver saves the day in a sleepy Arkansas suburb. I took two over, then went back for the other two. Tina had the baby out now and was bouncing him on her lap. Sarge was sitting right in the opening of the back doors with Opus, but Ophelia was standing on the bench seat. She'd taken me telling her to stay put seriously.

He started filling the cans. It didn't take long for the first two to be filled, and I capped them and carried them back. I had to make an empty spot by pushing the dogs out of the way. They were curious about the cans but one sniff and they backed off toward the bench.

"This isn't ideal," I told the boys.

"Sorry?" Javier asked.

I walked around the back door and started capping a third that he'd finished.

"Was talking to my dogs. We're trying to get out of town before the crazy stuff happens."

He looked up at me funny. I took the gas cap off the van and let it hang. "I paid for fifteen gallons roughly in the van."

"No problem," he said.

I capped the last can when it was filled and left the door open so the dogs could see out. They avoided the cans for now, but Sarge looked like he wanted to come my way.

"How's the smell up there?" I called.

"Can't smell the gas," Tina said. "I'm strapping little man in. He needed a change, and I burped him. He's happy now that he's got a bottle, but we're going to have to figure out food for him; he hasn't eaten much today."

"Want me to get him a banana from the cooler?" I asked.

"Actually, that'll work perfect. I'll sit back here with him while he eats."

So he doesn't choke, I thought to myself but didn't dare say aloud. Owen had never had a problem choking but with both of us being semi paranoid... we didn't always need to voice our fears. I got a banana out, and made sure all the cans were in place and wouldn't shift. Then I moved the cooler next to them so they couldn't slide side to side. Lastly, I put my big bugout bag in front of the cooler so it wouldn't slide forward. Sarge wasn't amused that I was blocking him in the van, but he let out a couple playful, irritated barks as I closed the back doors.

"You want me to top it off?" Javier asked as I came around the side, seeing him finishing the fill job.

"It's almost full already," I told him, "but I appreciate it."

I opened the side door and handed over the banana to Tina. Opus, Sarge, and Ophelia were staring out at me. I grinned, but the smile on Tina's face slipped as she took it from me. I turned to look where she was.

"Thank you, Javier," I told him, seeing that she was staring at him, her mouth open in confusion.

"No problem," he said, walking back toward the barn, crossing in front of the big green van.

"Let's get going," Tina said.

"That's weird, I..."

Tina gave the command for the dogs to be on guard. Opus sat up, looking around, and Ophelia got into the front passenger seat. Sarge sat at attention, a little behind the bench. I was confused, but closed the two side doors and went around and got in on my side. Ophelia had moved to sit in the middle, Opus next to Tina. Sarge was squished between Tina's legs and the car seat, so he ducked and got into Opus's spot.

"Go, ok?" Tina said, her voice nervous.

I put it in gear and started rolling, watching the gate shut behind them.

"Yeah, we've got a full tank, plus all the extra cans. What spooked you back there?' I asked her.

"I'm not sure. Let's bugout," Tina said, making me smile.

For once, I wasn't amused how she'd taken up the lingo. In the rearview mirror, she was wiping Owen's face with a wet wipe while he was shoving the banana in as far as he could.

20

TINA

Tina paid attention to Owen as he ate. The dogs didn't mind taking her spot, and Opus looked rather pleased with himself. The baby would break off a piece of banana with one hand and offer it to the dog first. Opus gave Tina a pleading look to which she answered with a shake of her head. Owen stuffed the piece into his mouth. Tina was uneasy, though. Javier from the towing company had made her uneasy. For a second there she'd thought he was one of the guys who'd tried to rob them the other night, but it had been dark and all she had to go on was the voice.

Tina wasn't sure if that was the right man or not, she didn't really get a good look at his face in the dark. She was pretty sure though that the voice of Javier was the voice of the man with the knife. When she'd locked eyes with him, there was no recognition or surprise. She didn't want to worry Rick, because she wasn't 100% sure for herself, just had a strong suspicion.

Sarge crawled into the middle between the two front seats because Tina was sitting in his spot. One was happily eating the remnant of a banana, and Opus sat there watching him, his head tilted the side. Ophelia, the princess of the clan, was sitting in the front seat where Tina normally sat. She'd been a little more clingy and a little more jealous lately than normal, but Tina knew that a lot of it probably had to do with them being out of town. She had to smile at the way Ophelia had adopted Rick. Opus was his buddy at first and still was, but Ophelia had definitely put a claim in.

"Daddy go bye-bye," Owen called through a mouthful of mush.

"Yeah, buddy," Rick said over his shoulder, "we're going to get outta here. Your mom is gonna plan me a route out of town, aren't you, Tina?"

"Yeah, just start heading north."

Tina reached down to her feet and started digging in the diaper bag, until she found a juice cup. Owen finished smacking his lips and held both sticky hands out for it.

"Here you go, buddy," Tina said as he made give me gestures with his little chubby fingers. "Don't drink it too fast and choke."

"Do I want to make my way toward I-75?" Rick asked.

Tina threw up her hands in frustration and sighed. The road they were on right now was already congested and bumper-to-bumper. She'd been dealing with the little tyrant and not listening to the radio or checking the app on her phone. She pulled her phone out and opened up the Waze app.

"It looks like heavy traffic going all the way up," Tina said after a few moments of using her thumb and zooming out. Then she directed the app to give them a route using back and secondary roads. That wasn't looking any better close to the big cities.

"You're better off staying on the main route for now," Tina told him. "I-75 seems to head straight west at this point. As much as I'd like to get away from the hurricane if we're going north, I think we ought to take 27 North if we want to avoid traffic."

"That sounds good to me," Rick told her. "It doesn't look like were gonna be going anywhere fast."

"What's everyone doing in the left turn lane?" Tina asked as the traffic seemed to be creeping's in one direction, with few cars going south.

"I don't know," Rick told her. "They probably open that lane up for an evacuation route?"

He started playing with the knobs on the radio, and soon a news report came on.

... all reports from the new projections have this hurricane up to a class IV. The governor hesitated and called for an evacuation of South Florida, but it just came in he's about to announce that. Unlike last time, he urges people to only fill up their gas tanks as they head north, to alleviate fuel shortages. Fuel companies already have trucks rolling south along the west coast of the state. We urge all citizens to listen for the directions if the governor does call for an evacuation ...

"Do you smell something?" Rick asked over his shoulder.

"It kind of smells..." Tina tapped her lips with her finger, "almost like antifreeze."

"That's what I thought," Rick said with a frown, putting his blinker on.

Rick could see Tina lean over, Owen grabbing her hand in case she decided she wanted to escape up front, but she could see what he was looking at as Rick put the blinker on. The dummy lights hadn't come on yet, but the temperature gauge was already swinging past the halfway mark, something the van had never done before.

"I can see a little bit of steam coming out of the hood," Rick said, pulling onto a side street to look at it.

AT LEAST IT WASN'T RAINING. OWEN WAS FUSSY, AND TINA was bouncing him on her hip. Sweat clung to her body and, even though the wind had picked up, it was nowhere near the howling winds they would get during a Michigan snowstorm. Instead of it being cold, it was muggy and humid. A promise of more weather and rain to come.

"There is a hole right through the radiator," Rick told her as a green puddle started collecting underneath the van.

Owen picked that moment to reach up and snatch Tina's glasses off her face. Tina switched him to her left side and gently pulled them out of his hands and put them back on with her right hand.

"Did a rock hit it?" she asked.

"No, come here and look at this," Rick told her, pointing.

Tina walked over and knelt down, seeing what Rick

was talking about. Green coolant leaked out of what looked like a hole that had been neatly punched right through the radiator. Rick took a rag and wiped a little bit.

"The hole didn't go all the way through," Tina said. "I can see a little bit of a pattern there."

"What did you see?" Rick asked her.

"It almost looked like a cross shape?" Tina said, standing back up, her knees popping.

"Mommy, I wan owwn," Owen said clearly.

"Not here, not on the side of the road," Tina said.

"Do you have anything to plug the leak?" Tina asked Rick.

"Yeah, I don't know if it would work though. It's bars leak. I can see if I can plug it from this side, or... We could always call AAA?"

"How about you get working on that, and I'll walk over to that Publix I can see. I'll pick up a couple gallons of water with the little man."

"We can't stay out in the heat for long," Rick told her, "the dogs will roast alive in there." He pointed to the dark van.

"If you've got enough coolant in the van without over-heating it, how about you pull forward about 25 or 30 feet so you're under the shade of that palm over there," she said, pointing ahead of the side road they'd pulled off onto.

Rick looked up and then down and knew that although it would work for right now, the sun would move and they'd be back in it again. Then again, he looked up at the sky and saw the clouds were blowing in and out. Was this what a hurricane looked like? He wasn't sure.

"Yeah, go ahead and go get some water. Get... maybe eight or ten gallons," he said, hoping it was enough.

Tina started walking, Owen a counter balance to the fear and anger she was feeling. Had it been Javier? As soon as they got on the road again she was going to mention it to Rick. She was still sorting her feelings out and didn't want to make an accusation when all she had to go on was the memory of a voice in the darkness and a vague outline of a face. The man she'd kicked? She knew that face well and if she saw it again, she was sure she could identify him.

"Wan owwwn," Owen repeated.

"Ok, Bubba," Tina said, putting him on his feet.

She waited while he wobbled and got his balance. He held up a chubby hand and took two of her fingers in his fist and followed her as fast as his little legs would let him.

"Grammy."

"She's on an airplane now. Headed back home. We'll be there soon too."

"Oppy?"

"Opus and puppies too," she told him, translating on the fly.

The grocery store doors opened automatically and cold air rushed out, cooling both of them immediately. Owen shivered, his little arms and legs bubbling up in goose bumps. Tina walked him over to a cart and boosted him up into the seat. She didn't bother with the buckles, but let Owen play with them while she made a beeline toward the back. Other people seemed to have the same idea. She saw shopping carts with bottled water headed up to the register, pushed by harried looking people.

"Did they call the evacuation yet?" an older gentleman asked, pushing a cart full of water and cat food.

"Not yet," Tina said, slowing. "Our van's radiator sprung a leak. Is there some place nearby to get it fixed or replaced?" Tina asked.

The man paused and put a gnarled finger to his chin, looking up in deep thought. "I reckon the closest place is Joe's Towing. He's a good 'um."

"Other than Joe's?" Tina asked.

"I think there's some of those tire shops that do more than tires and oil changes. I can't think of the name, but it's right up the road if you're headed north."

"We are, thank you," she said gratefully.

"Don't you worry 'bout this storm none. No way we'd get hit again so soon after the last one," he said, pointing at her. "And you, sir, keep your momma safe."

Owen crossed his arms and turned his head to the side, his skin turning a light shade of pink. Tina chuckled and the man made a face at Owen, sticking his tongue out. A smile crept over Owen's face, and he snickered.

"They still have a lot of water?" Tina asked.

"Better hurry," he told her and gave her a wave.

TINA FOUND THE WATER AISLE FULL OF PEOPLE. IT WASN'T A panic yet, but six or seven carts in that small of a space where soccer moms were picking cases of water up two at a time... Tina walked over to the section that hadn't been touched as much. The full one-gallon jugs. The store was almost out of the smaller bottled water, but the jugs were starting to go fast also. Tina knew Rick's van held a ton of coolant, because his oil change took twice as much oil as her truck did, and the motor was almost as obscenely big as the one in the motorhome that had brought them together.

She smiled at the memory and how he'd won her heart over that day when Opus and Rick had cleared the counter to stop the robber. That Superman punch hadn't been a pretty thing to watch, but Rick had landed it solidly enough to stun the man so Opus could finish his job.

"Dora?" Owen asked hopefully, pointing.

Tina snickered, she saw that he'd seen some theme juice boxes, with Dora The Explorer on them. She snagged a carton of those, then filled her cart up with water.

"One more thing we have to get. Hopefully your dad has everything he needs to fix the van."

"Owie go bubye?" he asked, his voice small.

"Yes, dear," she said softly.

His face scrunched up in a frown and his lower lip quivered.

"You're going bubye with me and Daddy, we're going to be with you. We're going on a car ride."

"Outside?" he asked hopefully.

"Yes, outside, then a car ride."

"Alright!" he said, slapping her hand in a one-man high five down low.

Tina grinned, realizing the crisis was averted. Now to find the automotive section.

21

RICK

I knew what that mark was as soon as I saw it for the first time. I opened the windows in the van all the way around and then the side doors. I gave all the dogs the command to stay, but Ophelia didn't listen to that and insisted on being right next to me. I'd gotten the van moved, and while Tina was inside I was digging through my milk crate of miscellaneous junk we kept on hand for the van. I now kept an extra battery behind the seat, not wanting a repeat of what had happened in Moab. But behind that was the milk crate, and I pulled it out and set it down on the concrete so I could see into it better. An extra serpentine belt, few quarts of oil, a gallon of antifreeze which I was about to use, some various hand tools, like the wrench I'd bought just for changing in a serpentine belt was there. Digging toward the bottom though, I finally found a small bottle of *Bars Leak*. I got that out and walked around to the front and cracked open the hood.

Either at the hardware store or at Joe's Towing, somebody had stuck a screwdriver into my radiator. I was sure of it, and it left me feeling really uneasy. Ophelia rubbed her left ear against my leg as I propped the hood up and slowly released the pressure on the radiator. I knew I could've poured it directly into the overflow tank and it would've gotten sucked into the radiator, but it was running hot and the overflow tank was the first place that was going to bubble over. I'd rather put the *Bars Leak* right in the radiator and see if I could do anything to get it stopped long enough to get to an auto parts store or somewhere to fix the van.

My one-ton Dodge held something like seven and a half, or eight quarts of oil and a couple gallons of antifreeze. After putting in the *Bars Leak* I put most of the antifreeze in and then put the cap on.

"Ophelia, go get in the front seat," I told my dog.

She listened and I walked around the driver's side and got in and started up the van. I got out and walked around the front. With the running van and a semi-pressurized system, the leak in the front started spurting. I cursed myself, and took the cap off of the antifreeze and then took the cap off the radiator again taking the extra pressure off. I had to give it enough time for the *Bars Leak* to work. Most of the damage had been done in the cooling fins, and I was hoping that the actual part where it was leaking could be closed off with just the *Bars Leak*. As long as I was able to keep adding fluid in a circulation through the van faster than it leaked out, I could, in theory, do this until I ran out of either liquid to put in or—

"Hey, help a girl unload?" Tina called.

"Dayee, we have wawa!" Owen said cheerfully.

I heard a scramble of claws and three dogs met her at the front of the van, the big doofus's tripping over each other in excitement.

Owen was still sitting in the front seat of the shopping cart, and there were ten gallons of water in the cart, along with some juice boxes with a cartoon character I loathed. I could see something else, but the label was turned away. I had a pretty good idea what it was, and I silently thanked the Lord again for bringing her into my life.

"I didn't even hear you coming up," I told her, placing a hand over my heart.

"Well I hope I didn't scare you," she said and gave me a smile.

"Just a little bit," I told her, "I didn't hear you sneaking up on me."

"Are we gonna be drinking this, or putting it in the radiator?" Tina asked.

"For right now, I'm gonna keep putting it in the radiator I think."

She pulled out another gallon of antifreeze. "And I thought you might need this," she said. "How bad is it?"

I looked back at the hole in the radiator, and the leaking fluid seemed to be slowing down.

"I poured in a bottle of *Bars Leak* and prayed it plugged the hole up enough for us to get back on the road again. Can you get the furry goofballs in the side doors so we're all out of the road?" I asked her, "And then peek in the driver side door and see if the engine's running hot or if it's okay?"

Tina nodded and gave a command in German. All three dogs took off and Owen laughed, clapping his hands together in delight. He mush mouthed something that sounded oddly like a command, and the dogs seemed to freeze and Tina turned her head sideways, cocked. He'd gotten it mostly right. I shivered, despite the heat and humidity. Thunder cracked overhead, making us all wince. Soon. The weather promised it was going to get ugly soon.

***

"ARE WE READY TO GO?" I ASKED TINA.

"Yup, everyone's all buckled in, and the furry kids are sitting in their own spots for once," Tina told me, looking around.

The *Bars Leak* seemed to have worked, but traffic had doubled in the time we'd been pulled over. The inside of the van was explosively hot, so it was with a bit of nervousness that I got out on the main road and merged into traffic, slowly heading north as I watched the temperature gauge. I kept the news on constantly, and Tina sat next to Owen, but was giving me news and updates on traffic conditions. We weren't on the road for more than ten minutes when the announcement came that the governor was going to order an evacuation. We'd already figured that, especially the way businesses were starting to shut down and people were getting on the road.

I had never been in a hurricane before, but seeing what the last one had done to the area, people were scurrying about as fast as they could. Because we were going so slow, we were able to see some of the residential areas off the main road, and homeowners were starting to board up their windows and doors. It was probably a process that all Floridians had gone through at some point, but it was something I'd only seen on the news. Until now.

"From what I'm seeing on the news," Tina told me without looking up, "traffic's getting snarled up ahead already."

"That's the way it looks for me too," I told her. "Any luck on finding an automotive parts store or someplace to get the van looked at?"

"There should be a Belle Tire up here on the right."

I found it about half a mile up on the right. Inch by inch, foot by foot, we crept forward. I turned the air conditioning off as it was blowing hot air in the van. Tina looked up at me sharply for a moment, but then nodded as she realized the van was starting to run hot again.

"Daddy, Owwie hot," my son called from the backseat.

"I know, buddy, we'll be pulled over here in another minute and I'll turn on the air-conditioning," I said over my shoulder.

"Rick," Tina said to me, "how bad is the temp getting?"

"We're over the three quarter way point right now, we're just starting to creep into the red zone. If traffic doesn't pick up—"

The car in front of me swerved hard to the left, cutting off someone in the middle lane. I heard a crunch as the front end of the car that was getting cut off hit the tail lights of the car that was going over. I had already steered to the right and touched my brakes hard. I wasn't far from the Belle Tire, so I pulled into a parking lot. Another flash of thunder almost distracted me from the turn, but I couldn't worry now. Traffic was going to come to an absolute crawl with that fender bender, and I was overheating.

"We're not there yet," Tina told me. "Is it getting too hot?" Her head was sideways, looking at the wreck that had happened just slightly south of us.

"I want to add a little water. Hold on, I'll park under the shade here," I said, noting some trees at the edge of the parking lot, though it wasn't a lot shadier than it was a second ago as darker clouds blew across the sun.

I'd pulled the van into a shopping mall parking lot. Calling it a shopping mall was being generous to be honest, because it was a glorified mini-mall with old beat up cars lining the front spaces near cutesy little boutiques. I got out after I turned off the van and walked to the back. I opened the back door only to have Sarge lick me in the face.

"Get off me," I scolded him. "I just want to do this and get out of the mugginess."

Sarge barked happily, his tail wagging his entire body. I got the two jugs of antifreeze out and headed toward the front of the van. Tina had already slid into my seat and was pulling the hood release. I had forgotten to do that; score one for the prepper's wife. I set the jugs down and then slowly cracked open the radiator cap, using my shirt to keep from burning my hand.

"Be careful," Tina called from my open window.

Steam poured out of the open radiator.

The sickly sweet smell of coolant hung in the air, and there was a puddle growing larger at my feet. I'd taken a peek at the hole, and whatever the *Bar Leak* had done it had been temporary. Without spilling too much, I poured the rest of the first jug into the radiator. I looked at the second jug that Tina had bought. It was the premix, 50/50 coolant and water. It was the universal kind, which my van wasn't picky about anyway. I started pouring that in, wishing I'd gotten my funnel out. I splashed some of the second gallon around, but I got it all in there. I could see there was at least an inch of space below the opening where the radiator cap was.

"Fire it up," I called to Tina.

"Got it, boss," she called back, with Owen yelling something unintelligible that ended in giggles.

The van fired up, and although the radiator was leaking, it wasn't leaking as hard as it had been before. I put the cap on, but not all the way. I wasn't going to pressurize the system until I had a chance to get the van looked at. I figured that was going to give me more time to get down the road.

I hurried up and got in the van, pushing Sarge out of the way as gently as I could. I could see Belle Tire, but the parking lots did not meet. I pulled out into traffic and crossed all my fingers and toes as I inched forward slowly.

"Dayee, we go bye?" Owen asked from the backseat.

"Yeah buddy, we're about to go bye-bye."

"You let your daddy concentrate on driving," Tina said, turning to face the little man.

Ophelia pushed past Sarge in the space between the front seats and she put her head on my right leg. If I'd been driving a stick shift this wouldn't have been possible, but she must have been feeling my anxiety. I put my hand on her head and started scratching her ears. I saw in the rearview mirror Opus watching me, his big brown eyes calm and steady. Behind me where the accident had happened, cars were just now starting to move as both vehicles were finally able to pull into the parking lot I had just vacated.

It took two minutes of watching the temperature gauge start climbing into the hot zone again before I was able to pull into the tire shop.

"I've got the baby and the dogs," Tina said. "I'm going to go give them a quick walk."

"Sounds good to me, I'm going to go inside and see what they can do.

THE NEWS WASN'T GOOD. TINA TOOK ALL THREE DOGS ON leashes and put on Owen's dinosaur backpack. For all intents and purposes he was on a leash himself, and they roamed around the grassy area on the back of the tire place. I gritted my teeth at the news. They could order the part in, but it wouldn't be in until tomorrow, right when this area was about to get busy with the evacuation. That was when I decided to change tactics.

"If you can get me the part," I told the sales manager, "I can put it in myself. If you can get me the part and if someone's willing to stay and help me put it in or install it for me, I'll make sure they're fairly compensated."

"That doesn't leave us much time to do our own evacuation. As we saw with the last big hurricane to have an evacuation order isn't just a polite suggestion, it's an order."

"What about if I buy a plane ticket out of here for whoever sticks around?"

The sales manager hesitated for a moment, then looked at me. "Why can't you just fly back?"

"Because I've got three German Shepherds, my wife, and a baby. I could get the humans on the plane easily enough, but I haven't been able to find any airline that's able to take the dogs on short notice like this. I can't leave them behind, they're family too," I said, looking outside, Pat following my gaze.

Tina had been checking options while the mechanics here had looked at it. The hole was too big for a simple soldering patch. I wasn't an expert on this by any means, but I thought the radiator was toast. The screwdriver had pushed almost entirely through the radiator. I hadn't had a chance to tell Tina my suspicions and made a mental note to make sure I did that as soon as I could.

"You know, I don't know if this will help, but there is a junkyard not too far from here. If you're willing to do the install yourself... We're not allowed to put in parts like that, warranty issues and liability reasons. In theory a person could buy a radiator, and have it back here in a couple hours. Maybe less if the part is already pulled off the vehicle..."

"Do you happen to have the phone number of the salvage yard?" I asked him.

He pulled out his cell phone, hit a couple of buttons, and made a call.

"Hey, George, this is Patrick down here... Yeah hey, I need a radiator for a 97 Dodge Ram van. Yeah, the big one-ton. Yeah, can you pull one out? Oh come on... Get one of the boys to go pull it real quick, I'm sending someone over. I'd consider it a personal favor."

"Tell him I'll pay extra if he has it out by the time I get an Uber over there," I interrupted.

"You hear that? Guy's willing to pay extra if you go yank it right now. Uh huh, I hear you. Yeah, if you can get on that; appreciate it. I'll either flag a taxi for him or call him an Uber or something. Yeah, he's a writer guy that my wife likes to read—"

My mouth dropped open and I started chuckling. I listened to the rest of the conversation while pulling out my own cell phone to download the Uber app. Despite being familiar with it I'd never used it myself. One more thing Annette had beaten me to try first.

"I'll just call you a cab," the sales manager said.

I held my hand out. "I really appreciate this," I told him as we shook.

"You got tools?" he asked me.

"I should," I told him.

He was already dialing another phone number and asked for a customer pickup and gave the address.

"So your wife reads my books?" I asked him.

"Yeah, she says you've really changed the genre. I tried to read one of them once. Wasn't for me, but the girls seem to get worked up about it. So I keep buying them for her. Might need you to sign a couple for me to give to her."

I chuckled, "Sure thing and thanks; it helps keep me rolling... Unless we're under an evacuation order and someone sticks a screwdriver through my radiator."

"I was going to ask you about that, you know where it happened?"

"Yeah, I think it happened at Joe's Towing. I was buying gas and I don't want to make accusations but... I wasn't leaking radiator fluid until after I'd been there."

"There's a couple of people who work for Joe that have... Just be careful," he finished, typing something up on his computer.

"I better get out there and let Tina know. Are they okay coming in here and cooling down?" I asked him.

"Yeah, and tell her feel free to bring the dogs too, as long as they are well-behaved."

Little did he know.

22

TINA & OPUS

Opus could smell the ozone in the air. He didn't know what that word meant, but it was the funny tingly smell after lightning. Instead of a huge storm, there seemed to be a lot of wind. He let out a low growl, and Sarge barreled up to him. Opus made a sneezing sound and then rubbed his head on the baby's shoulder. Sarge sat down, his head cocked.

Ophelia watched her mate, but she was pacing nervously, looking at the building that the human Rick had gone into. She felt an overwhelming need to make sure he didn't get himself into trouble. Opus knew that the human Rick was good at finding trouble, but he seemed to come out ok. Especially when he had Opus's entire family taking care of him and his.

"Oppy!" Owen said, petting Opus' head and grabbing a handful of ear, yanking.

Opus shook his head, breaking the grip, and put one

paw up. Owen laughed and tried to put his own foot up and fell backward on his padded rear end. Opus wasn't sure why this human felt the need to catch his waste and hold it close to his body, but his humans kept dressing him that way. One more mystery and one more reason why humans needed a firm and thoughtful owner.

"Hey!" Rick called, coming out of the roll-up glass door that the van was being backed out of.

Ophelia took off like a shot, followed by Sarge. The human Tina called a halt just as Opus was about to run over and make sure nothing had happened to his person, and Opus stopped, as did the others.

"Dayee!" Owen called as Rick jogged over, followed by the dogs.

"Hey, buddy," he said, sitting down in the rough grass.

Opus watched as everyone gathered near while a strange human parked the van on the side of the building.

TINA WASN'T HAPPY WITH THE NEWS SHE'D JUST GOTTEN. IT was getting late in the day, and she'd relentlessly been checking airlines for cancellations. She had memorized Rick's debit card numbers and three digit code on the back in case she'd ever needed it. She was almost in a panic mode as she saw that he didn't have an outright grin on his face.

"They can't get it in in time?" she asked after he'd sat down and the dogs had encircled them.

"No, but the manager found one at a salvage yard. As soon as the taxi gets here, I'm going to pick it up. I should be able to put it in no problem when I get back."

"Why are you putting it in?" Tina asked.

"Warranty and liability reasons," Rick told her.

"You mean, they won't put in a used part and..."

"Right," Rick told her, knowing where she was going with it. "I'll leave the keys with you guys. Pat, the sales manager, said you five can go inside and cool off while you wait. They have a TV, microwave, and a bathroom."

"That..." Tina said, standing up and scooping up Owen, "sounds like the best thing I've heard in the last ten minutes. So they really have the part?"

"They really have the part," Rick told her. "They're pulling it as we speak."

He pulled open his wallet and pressed a few bills into her hand. She looked down to see they were $100 bills.

"Just in case you need anything or... I'm sorry I don't have smaller change."

"I've got money," Tina said with a grin, but pocketed it, despite a squirming Owen.

A yellow taxi inched alongside the road, it's blinker on. Tina nodded to it.

"Ah, looks like my ride. Depending on traffic, I should be back soon."

"I love you," Tina called.

"Love you both more," he shot back and started walking. Opus and Ophelia started walking beside him.

"You can't go with him," Tina called, making Rick stop and turn.

"They should stay here," Rick told her.

Ophelia whined and Opus made a disgusted sound, sneezing repeatedly.

Rick sighed, "Let me make sure the cab driver doesn't have an issue," he said as the car started to park, but then must have noticed them, because it turned in their direction.

"You the ones going to the scrapyard?" the cabbie asked through a window that was cracked open.

"Yeah, is it ok if I bring—"

"I can't fit six of you's in here," he said, with a heavy Jersey accent.

"Just me and one of these goofballs is all?" Rick asked.

"Oh, yeah sure. I'm only rated for five though, and I really can only fit three. As long as the dog doesn't shit all over the place, I'm fine."

"It!" Owen cried happily, making both parents wince.

"Ok," Rick said, opening the backdoor.

Opus jumped in, turning back to look at Ophelia, almost daring her in a glance to try to get in. Rick grinned at the antics.

"Ophelia, you stay here and make sure Sarge behaves. I need you to take care of Tina and Owen for me while I'm gone."

Ophelia audibly whined again, but Tina walked over, petting her. Sarge stayed sitting where he'd come to rest, panting in the late afternoon heat.

"You sure you don't want to take her instead?" Tina asked. "She's been really anxious about being away from you lately."

"I know," Rick told her. "I... It doesn't matter to me, or they all can stay with you?"

"Meter's running," the cabbie said.

"Oh, go ahead. She'll be fine."

Rick gave them both a quick kiss on the forehead and got in the cab, slamming the door. They watched as it pulled out of the parking lot, to nearly come to a standstill as they merged into northbound traffic. Tina mused that it might take a while to get there, but the trip back would be easy as everyone seemed to be heading north.

"Let's go inside and cool off," she said.

RIGHT AWAY, PATRICK SHOWED THEM TO THE LOUNGE AREA. The shop stayed open until 6pm, but they were staying later tonight to try to finish as many jobs as possible. Still, the place was mostly silent except for the drone of the weather channel on TV and the sound of air tools being used.

"Patrick?" Tina asked as he had turned to leave the waiting area.

"Yes, ma'am?" he said, turning, surprised to see a dog on either side of her and Owen.

"I know you can't install the radiator, but I was thinking... do you have someone to spare who could pull out the old one? That'd save us some time and we can get on the road faster?"

"That's not a bad idea. Actually, I've got a guy who's free right now. No warranty on a tear out, but I'll have him label all the parts and where they go in Ziploc baggies if that'd work?"

"I'm sure that'd be perfect. Rick knows what he's doing. I probably could as well, but I'm not strong enough to do some of that stuff. Short girl problems."

Ophelia whined, then stuck her nose in Tina's side, then rubbed her head against her.

"That won't be a problem," Patrick said, then walked past the glass door into the mechanics area, calling somebody over.

"I forgot to get the keys from Rick," Tina told Owen.

Lightning flashed outside and thunder rolled immediately. Owen startled so badly, when he turned to look outside, he almost fell off the chair he'd been standing on. Sarge already had his head down, but moved it just as Tina and Owen were in motion. Owen's butt impacted with the edge of the chair and Sarge's head just as Tina scooped him out of the air.

Owen let out a surprised squall and started to cry. Tina held him close, rocking slowly. "It's ok, buddy, you didn't fall, shhhhhh."

Sarge got off the chair and stretched, sniffing the air. Once again, rain started falling, but the wind seemed to have died back.

"Wan Dayee," Owen said, squirming.

She held him close. "I do too. Listen, do you hear that?" she asked as the sound of a familiar motor fired up and pulled in the last bay, farthest away from them?

"Dayee?" Owen said, looking as the behemoth van was pulled inside.

"No, not yet. He'll be back soon."

"I wan Dayee!"

Tina sighed and put him back in his seat and bent over to dig in his diaper bag she'd brought in with her for snacks or a toy.

23

RICK

"So what you getting at the scrapyard?" the cabbie asked.

"My radiator sprung a leak," I lied. "I need to get it put in before tomorrow's evacuation goes into effect."

"Sounds like a good idea. That last hurricane has everybody worried. I had those fancy storm shutters put on after the last one. Locked my house up tight yesterday, just in case."

"You going to ride out the storm?" I asked him, incredulous.

"That's right, I got plenty of work to do, people to get to the airports. I've never been married, no kids, and I know where to go inland on higher ground when these things happen. This cab is a newer one, I have three payments left. Just staying around when people are wanting to head to places before a big event like this... I could pay this thing off in the next day or two."

"You an independent?" I asked him, curious, because he had a company logo on the outside of the cab.

"Naw, I own this chain. Too cheap to bring in extra drivers for hazard pay. I let the guys off who wanted tonight off, but I'm still making money any way I can."

I grinned at that. He wasn't being greedy, just realistic.

"Who's your furry buddy back there?" he asked.

"Opus," I told him, and hearing his name, Opus snapped to attention.

"Opus, Hm... like a masterpiece type of thing?"

"I guess so. My wife named him," I said. "Hey, can you stick around the junk yard and give me a ride back?"

"As long as you're paying, I have no beefs," he said, grinning in the rearview mirror.

I pulled my wallet out and dropped $100 through the partition. He picked it up with his right hand without looking, then brought it up to his face. He grinned and stuffed it in his shirt pocket, then put the blinker on. I looked and we'd traveled the eight miles to the scrapyard. When I looked at my watch, I saw that it had taken a lot longer than I'd been expecting.

"This sort of covers the first leg," the cabbie told me, "I'll get you an exact price when we get back to the tire shop."

"Thanks," I told him as we pulled in and he put it in park. "We'll both be right back in a second."

THERE WERE TWO RADIATORS WAITING FOR US AT THE counter when I walked in. There were very few passenger vehicles that had a motor as large as mine. I walked up to a guy who was gnawing on a stub of a cigar, his sleeveless shirt covered in grease. His hair was close cropped and shot through with silver. I put him to be in his sixties, judging by the lines on his face. Still though, he looked to be in great shape.

"Help you?" he asked, looking down at Opus.

"Patrick called here about getting me a radiator for a Dodge Ram Van?" I said, seeing the name tag that showed the name George.

"Yup, got two to choose from," he said, hooking a thumb at the two on the counter. "I pulled both. Haven't pressure checked either of them though. Neither looks like it has coolant stains coming from any of the fins or welds. Florida vehicles. Take your pick, $150."

Opus chuffed, and I put my hand down to pat him on the head.

I lifted one up on the counter, looking at the front and back, noting the mounting brackets looked to be in the exact same spot mine were in. Then I checked out the other. I took a deep breath and considered last time I'd been stuck with the van. Bad things had happened, and I didn't want to ever be in that situation again, no matter what. Two is one and one is none... and only having one was the reason I was in here. Of all the things I'd put away for my van, a radiator was the last thing I'd expected to need a spare of. Now that I thought about it, a water pump would have been good to store also...

"I'll take both," I said, surprising the man.

Opus made a growling sound, but his tail wagged as I pulled my wallet out. He apparently agreed with my sentiment. I pulled out three one hundred dollar bills and put them on the counter. "Any tax?" I asked.

The man looked side to side then shook his head, grabbing the bills. "Cash sales are final, no refunds."

"That's ok, we're heading out tonight," I told him, "before the evacuation."

"Everybody losing their damned minds about this hurricane suddenly. Ain't like it's the first to hit down here."

"Yeah, I guess the last one has people jumpy," I said.

He grunted again and pocketed the money then picked up one of the radiators. "That your cab?" he asked, nodding outside.

"Yeah," I told him, picking up the other radiator.

"I'll give you a hand. Grab that sheet of cardboard there." He nodded to a half clean one leaned against the side of the counter.

I did, almost losing my grip, but was able to juggle it. He followed me out, and seeing both of us, the cabbie popped the trunk. He got out and was about to object when George put the clean side of the cardboard down in the trunk, then his radiator. Then he folded over the cardboard and loaded the radiator I had been holding. Opus watched us from several feet back.

"That does it, thanks," I said, holding out my hand.

"You be safe," George said, shaking mine. "Tell Patrick to have his wife and kids give me a shout when they get back into town, my Susie has been missing them."

"I will," I said, not quite sure what that meant, but figured these two knew each other the way the hardware guy had known Joe's Towing.

It was just a little after closing at the tire shop when we pulled in. Traffic had picked up quite a bit. The trip south that had looked easier before took almost as long as it did getting there. We had to wait almost five minutes with the blinker on to turn in before traffic would stop enough for us to sneak in. I peeled another bill out of my wallet, noting that I was tipping him well. I saw the van at the far end in front of one of the roll up doors. I pointed, and he pulled over there.

"Thanks!" I told him as he popped the trunk.

"No problem. Feel free to call us again," the cabbie said, patting his breast pocket where the cash resided.

Opus let out a sharp bark and followed me.

"I'm kind of hoping I won't need to," I said, pulling the first radiator out and leaned it up against the tire of the van before going back for the second one and cardboard.

"Thanks!" the cabbie called after I closed the trunk.

"No problem," I called as he took off.

"I wonder where your mom is?" I asked Opus, seeing the lights of the shop off.

Opus was silent as normal, so I walked over, opening the side door. Sarge and Ophelia barreled out, swarming me and sniffing me all over. I could see Owen's diaper bag on the passenger seat. What I didn't see was my wife and son.

"That's weird. Where's your mom?" I asked them all.

Sarge barked and Ophelia sat down, staring at me. Opus sniffed at each of them, his tail wagging.

"Let's go check and see if they're still in the office," I told the three fuzzy kids.

I closed the side doors and looked at the almost empty lot. I decided to leave the radiators out and walked to the office. Even though the windows inside the shop were dark, I tried the door anyway. It was locked. I could see the blinking light of a security panel for the alarms. It was armed.

"Where are they?" I asked.

Ophelia whined and turned in a nervous circle. I pulled out my phone and started walking toward the van. I got most of the way there when I saw I had a text message from Tina.

Owen was restless, and we got hungry. I cracked the windows and made sure the furry kids had food and water. I tried to take them with us but not dog-friendly business. Meet us up the road at the golden arches where we'll be eating French fries and playing in the plastic jungle gym. Oh! I had the guys take the old radiator out to save you time. Parts are labeled and on the seat. Old radiator is next to dumpster if you need it. Weather seems to be getting worse on the radar and news. Love you!

"I love you too," I said aloud as I thumbed the same words in my phone.

I'll pick you two up soon. Get food for me and Opus please.

I opened the driver's side door of the van, wincing at the fact it was unlocked. I reached under the driver's seat and found the locked box. I pulled it out and put in the combination and opened it, to see my pistol was still locked up safely. So were the keys to the van. I nearly swooned in relief, then pulled the hood latch. Tina had a spare set of keys and might have thought I had my set with me. I climbed in and saw my computer bag behind my seat was untouched. I got out and went to the back with my keys and unlocked the back. I had a basic set of hand tools there, more than enough to change a radiator. I took my small kit to the front of the van and popped the hood.

They really had done a lot to save me time. I saw Ziploc bags of nuts and bolts labeled on the air filter and the empty spot where the radiator was. I grinned.

IT TOOK SOME FINAGLING AND BUSTED KNUCKLES, BUT I WAS mostly done with putting the radiator in when two things happened. The sun started going down and it started to rain again. This time, it wasn't the warm rain, it soaked me and chilled me as the wind started to pick up. Opus and others had elected to get in the side door of the van and were sprawled out, watching and waiting. The last thing for me to do was to add more coolant. I had used up all I had getting here, but I knew I had enough water for sure. I knew water was actually a better coolant, but it could freeze. That's why we didn't run straight water up north, but as a temporary thing I wouldn't hesitate. I probably had enough regular coolant in the system to survive a cold night without cracking my block, not that I had to worry about that.

"Just have to pour some of this in, start it up and top it off," I told Opus as I opened the back doors and got two gallons of water out. "Or I could just leave the cap off for ten minutes the way this is coming down," I grumbled, closing it back up before all our stuff got soaked.

I'd loaded the second radiator behind the back seat earlier when I'd dug out some tools. I couldn't wait to pick up Tina and Owen and get on the road. There had been a steady sound of traffic and as I poured the water into the radiator, I saw a constant stream of red brake lights. I prayed I had every clamp on tight because as wet as things were right now, I'd never be able to tell if I had a major leak. I left the radiator cap off and went and started the motor.

Thunder and lightning crashed overhead, but the van fired right up. I went back to the front of the van and watched air bubbles come out of the radiator as the water was pumped through the system. I knew from past experience that after doing something like this, you sometimes had to let it go for five to ten minutes to get all the air out and top off the radiator. I wasn't worried about the top off, but the wind and rain were starting to freeze me. I was sure it was sixty-five or seventy-five degrees, but I was soaked and the wind seemed to make it feel much, much colder than it was.

Opus barked happily, and I looked around the side of the hood to see him in the driver's seat. I grinned and waited, pouring the rest of the water in the radiator before putting the cap on and closing the hood.

"Get over," I said, opening my door.

Opus sneezed and got in the passenger side as I dropped the empty containers in the middle. "Let's go to the arches and pick up your mom so we can get out of here!"

I DIDN'T HAVE FAR TO GO AND WATCHED THE NEEDLE AS THE van heated up. So far, so good. Until... Red and blue lights were what I saw as I pulled into the McDonald's. Cops and an ambulance. My heart dropped and I prayed for the first time in years. I put my blinker on and was pulling in when a policeman tried to wave me not to. I ignored his frantic waving and pulled up short, rolling my window down.

"We've shut it down for an investigation," he yelled at me, his voice angry.

"My wife and son are here," I told him.

"Your wife and... Sir, please park over here," he said, waving at another cop and pointing to a spot next to the ambulance.

My heart was going a thousand miles an hour, threatening to explode. My mouth was dry and I realized that for the very first time in my life, I was more scared than any other time than I could remember. I saw another cop take the place of the guy who flagged me over. I parked and kept my window down as he ran over to the side.

"Sir, what's your wife and son's name?"

"Tina and Owen. Owen's a little over two, and my wife's about five-feet-nothing, glasses, pixie haircut—"

"Owen?" he said, mumbling something into the microphone on his shoulder.

"Yes, he's two," I said loudly, so I could be heard over the wind.

"Sir, please come with me," he said, getting out.

I did, and Ophelia jumped out. Opus and Sarge tried

to but the policeman's eyes got huge when he saw three hundred pounds of fur staring at him.

"You two watch the van for me, I'll be back," I said, pushing both gently and closing the passenger side door.

"Your dog there, she's not mean is she?" he asked, nervous.

"She's a trained S&R police dog," I told him. "She's got a little separation anxiety when she isn't around me. Is it ok?"

"Would your son know the dog?" the policeman asked.

"Oh yeah," I said, my heart leaping at that. They were here! "The younger goofball is Sarge, Owen's dog."

My heart dropped when he knocked on the back of the ambulance and they opened the door. He gestured for me to stand next to him. I tried, but Ophelia muscled her way between both of us and hopped in. The EMTs shouted in surprise, but I heard Owen's voice.

"Ofie! Dayee!" he screamed gleefully.

I saw him walking toward me, his feet moving faster than his body. The EMT caught him before he could fall, but I wrapped my arms around him and held him tight.

"Owen, you ok, buddy?" I asked, pushing him back slightly so I could look him over.

Ophelia barked happily, licking Owen on the side of the head before getting me.

"Where's your mom?" I asked him.

"Momma go bye?" Owen asked me.

I saw two EMTs but no Tina. The cop next to me coughed and motioned to me.

"We were called because at first it appeared that

Owen was abandoned here. We've done a check and he's healthy. We were about ready to put his picture on the news, but he's obviously... I mean, you have official birth certificate and records on you?"

"Yes, we traveled down here from Michigan. I brought them with me for the cruise. Where's my wife?"

"Let's go inside, out of the rain. I'm not sure if they'll let you bring a dog in, but this time, we might have to make an exception," he said as Owen wrapped his arms around Ophelia tightly, working his fingers deep into her fur.

24

TINA

S *tupid!*
Her memory was fuzzy, and she struggled with consciousness...

Tina knew when Javier and his partner walked in that it was no coincidence. They locked eyes with her and the man she'd stomped made a shooting motion at the both of them. Then he hooked his finger, telling her silently to come toward the glass door separating the play area from the rest of the restaurant. She didn't want to, and was instead reaching for her phone when Javier pulled up his shirt, showing her a chromed pistol. She froze, hearing Owen's laughter behind her as he played in the ball pit.

Then things got confusing. She knew that they spoke and that threats were made. She hoped that they hadn't noticed the tow-headed toddler behind her because they paid him no attention. She'd cried as softly as possible, remembering their threats to kill her here if she made a scene and, not wanting Owen to get hurt, she did what she could to comply. She'd handed over her purse where they took her phone and her wallet with all her cards and cash. They found and pocketed the .380 she kept in there as well, snickering between themselves.

She turned her head as Owen decided to come up and say hi. She'd tried to tell him to go back to play, but Javier grabbed her arm tightly.

"He'll be fine, we're just going to teach you not to mess with us," he had said, handing her a white pill.

"What's this?" she'd asked.

"What I should have had put in your drink," Javier's partner said, "instead of your husband's. Now it's time to pay you back. Don't worry, you won't remember anything tomorrow."

"Heh, I will," the man she'd stomped said, grinning maliciously.

Tina almost forgot everything as a blind panic started to over take her.

No, not again! Never!

Javier pulled the gun out of his waistband and pointed it under the table at Owen. Tina's heart nearly broke. She would endure anything. She could shut it out, she'd done it before.

"You won't hurt him," she said, statement not a question.

"Just you and us," Javier said.

She'd taken the pill and dry swallowed it.

"I can't just leave him here," she'd told them.

"Better than being dead, isn't it?"

The tears flowed, harder than she'd expected.

SHE HAD FELT SOMEBODY PAWING AT HER CLOTHING, hearing the fabric rip. She felt drunk, everything was fuzzy. She'd slumped slightly and somebody pushed her so her back was against something rough. Brick? She opened her eyes and saw a familiar stranger, yanking at the front of her shirt. Javier? She reacted without thinking, a result of constant training and practice ever since Owen had been born. She pulled him closer to her and he'd greedily moved in thinking in her drugged state she was giving in.

Her knee came up. It had felt like slow motion to Tina, but she'd connected and Javier's breath had left him in a rush. He leaned forward. She managed to grab the back of his head and smash it against first one knee, then another. His head rocked back, and she threw a rabbit punch into his throat, dropping him before she stumbled and fell. Javier's friend rushed in, and she went down under his weight. That was when she saw a flash of chrome to the right as his weight knocked the wind out of her lungs.

THE GUN!

She reached, her vision swaying. A heavy punch hit her in the side of the head, and for a moment she blacked out. She heard scrambling a moment later and the weight lifted off of her. She gasped for breath as a man cursed and retched somewhere nearby. Her hand reached out and she felt a cold shape in the darkness. She opened her eyes, realizing that she'd grabbed the slide of a cheap pistol and saw Javier's buddy undoing his belt. His eyes were on her semi exposed chest and not her hand. His eyes opened in surprise when the bore of the .45 was pointing his way.

Tina started firing.

25

RICK

The owner was pulling the security tapes already, and we were heading into the McDonald's with Owen and Ophelia when we heard the gunshots.

"Get down," Officer Hanson said, pushing me and Owen behind the brickwork McDonald's was known for.

"Shots, three or four blocks away," the cop who was waving traffic back called.

"Momma?" Owen asked.

I knew what I had to do. Ophelia was close to me, but I needed at least one more. I ignored Officer Hanson's yells as I rushed to the van, yelling commands to Opus. Ophelia kept pace next to me until I made it to the door. Both Sarge and Opus nearly knocked me and Owen over as they rushed out of the van.

"Go find Tina," I told Ophelia, then snarled something in German to Opus who suddenly went very still.

For once, Sarge looked serious as well. "Go find. Now. Protect," is what I think the command translated to. I

pointed in the sound of the shots and three of them took off at a dead run, Sarge barking almost nonstop like a hunting dog.

"What the hell?" two officers said, rushing to me.

"I told you, Ophelia is a S&R dog. If that's my wife, they'll track her and protect her from whatever's going on," I said, starting to follow.

"You can't go that way, this is a police matter."

I heard Sarge or Opus bay like a coon hound, and I pushed my way past both of them in a fast walk. "Try to stop me."

"Can you run?" a younger cop asked, walking briskly in stride with Hanson.

"We can't rush in there recklessly, and he's got a kid."

"EMTs are ready to roll, and we have backup coming from two other directions. My money is on the dogs, if it's her."

"You guys better keep up," I said, cradling Owen close to me as I moved slowly, using cars and buildings as cover, listening as my team of shepherds made as much noise as the rain and the wind. "They won't listen to anybody but me. I'm going."

OPUS AND SARGE WERE BLOODY WHEN WE GOT THERE. When I saw Tina, I wanted to tear the throat out of the two men I recognized. The hardware store and the towing shop. Tina's top was half torn, half open, and she was covered in blood from her neck to waist. She moaned, rocking side to side, her hands on her head. I was going to rush over, but the EMTs beat me there. Both Sarge and Opus had chewed on a semi-conscious man who was holding his throat. Ophelia stood over a chromed 1911, her fangs out, snarling louder than anybody else. The man had his back against the wall of an old Sunoco and every time he moved, Opus and Sarge would dart in, fangs barred.

"Nein," I said loudly.

All three of them sat down, but I barely saw it. All that blood on Tina but—

"Blood isn't hers," an EMT said over his shoulder, "breathing and heart rate normal."

He took a pen light out of his pocket and pried open an eyelid. "Looks drugged or drunk, possible concussion."

"Is she... I mean..."

"Male suspect is not responsive, suspect two needs medical attention, but not as much as her. We don't know if this is an OD or—"

"They roofied her," I said.

The officer looked up at me sharply. "How do you know?" he asked me.

"They got me a few nights back, trying to rob me. Tina fought them off. We didn't call the police at first, but the bar—"

"I heard about that call. You recognize these guys?" Hanson asked.

"That guy's name is Javier," I said, the tears running freely down my face. "He works at Joe's Towing. Other guy who was chewed on works at the hardware store a

while back. These have to be the guys who tried to rob us."

"That sounds…"

"It fits," the EMT said "Ma'am, can you hear me?" He gently shook Tina.

Her eyes swam open, but her movements and speech were drunken.

"Owen, Rick?" she asked.

The dogs made it half a second before I did, Ophelia pushing the EMT out of the way to lay her head in Tina's armpit.

"Oh, sweet girl. You found me."

Ophelia chuffed as Opus and Sarge sniffed her, before Opus sat down next to her, grumbling at the EMT. I sat down next to them, Owen in my arms crying for his mom. The cops were already busy checking the two men, taking control of the dropped gun, cuffing the one suspect and a second EMT crew started working on the man who was face down in a growing pool of blood.

OWEN HAD SOBBED HIMSELF TO SLEEP ON MY SHOULDER AS we walked back to the van. He'd been scared, alone, and then saw his mom almost passed out. I would have ridden with her in the ambulance, but I had the three dogs and the baby. One of the officers had offered to ride with Tina, but the priority was the man she had shot. Somehow she'd beaten the first one and wrestled the gun away from the second one. She'd been semi-conscious when the EMTs loaded her up and had told me she loved me.

"AHH, YOU MUST BE RICK," DOCTOR SORENSON SAID, coming into the crowded waiting room, noting a sleeping Owen and three dogs in tow.

"Yes," I said standing up, "how's my wife?"

"She's fine," Doctor Soren said, checking a clipboard. "We administered Flumazenil as soon as possible, but we're monitoring her under concussion protocols."

"I hear she put up one hell of a fight," I said, feeling relieved.

"You should see the other guys."

"You mean the one guy made it?" I asked.

"So far. He's in surgery, but the bullet nicked his heart. The cardiac surgeons have been working nonstop. Even if he makes it through that, he's going to have a couple more surgeries to go."

"What about the other guy?" I asked him.

"Bruised throat and groin. Concussion, needs stitches from where your dogs pulled him away from Tina. Cops have already arrested him, but he hasn't been medically discharged yet."

I didn't know if I was relieved that so far everyone was alive or not. For what they had tried to do and nearly done... part of me wanted them dead. I knew about Tina's ex, but he wasn't the only monster who haunted her dreams and I knew at some point we were going to have to have an awkward talk. I'd never pressed her on it, and I probably wouldn't now unless she… we… needed to. The wind was picking up. It howled and seemingly rattled the windows.

"How long will she be in here?" I asked him.

"We need to hold her for observation while the Rohypnol is flushed from her system and the Flumazenil does its work, and a bad concussion like hers is usually a twenty-four-hour wait."

"What about the evacuation?" I asked him, terrified.

"We're on the fourth floor, the hospital was built on high ground and at my last count, I've sheltered here for the last dozen or two hurricanes."

"Dozen or two?" I asked him, "Irene…?"

"Kept us busy, but we were fine. When you live in Florida, you tend to be prepared for this kind of thing. Day after tomorrow is when the hurricane hits… So maybe this time tomorrow night I could write the discharge, but it might be better to keep her an extra day for observation. The punch to the head bounced her skull off the wall or asphalt."

"I… really?" I said, feeling lost.

"When's the last time you slept?" he asked me.

"This morning, but I get up stupid early," I said, wondering if I could see her.

"Good, let me show you where you can take the dogs to do their business and then I'll take you to the room your wife's going to be in."

I grabbed my backpack, and Doctor Sorenson got the diaper bag before I could shift Owen to pick it up. It had to be late now. Middle of the night late.

"Come on, Opus, get the fam in line," I told him.

Opus chuffed and Ophelia and Sarge got up, stretching from where they'd been lightly snoozing. I'd used baby wipes to clean the blood off the boys' muzzles and was surprised that the ER doc had been alerted that I had two service dogs and a S&R dog coming inside. I always kept a few pounds worth of dry kibble for the dogs in my go bag, and judging by the growling in their stomachs I was hearing, they would appreciate it soon. I just didn't know the rules and regs about them in a hospital like Tina did. She'd been the one to get Opus certified and taken the classes and volunteered.

"They listen rather well. Almost like they know what you said to them exactly," the doc said, opening up a door after swiping his badge.

"You might think I'm crazy, but they really do. Shepherds are one of the smartest breeds, and I think Opus here has about three hundred words he can understand if I remember right. I just talk to him and he generally gets the idea."

"Anthropomorphism," Doc Sorenson said without looking up, muttering to himself.

"Ophelia, that diaper bag is looking heavy and the Doc is tired," I said.

She walked faster than the other two and nudged his hand holding the bag. He stopped and turned, looking at me. I grinned back and motioned to the floor. He lowered the bag, and Ophelia took the handles in her jaws. She wasn't as tall as Opus and Sarge, but she was able to lift it up off the floor and looked at me expectantly.

"Follow the doc, I guess," I told her.

Doc looked at me, his eyebrows almost touching his

hairline. He turned and started walking, his head looking back. Ophelia walked right behind him. Opus and Sarge had their tongues hanging out the sides of their mouths in what I could swear was silent laughter.

"I'll be dipped in—"

Sarge barked once and the doc stopped again, turning.

"I'm sorry I doubted you, I can take the bag," he said, petting Ophelia on the head.

Her tail wagged, and she put the bag down and licked his hand. He put it down and she took the opportunity to jump up and lick him on the face. He laughed in surprise and gently pushed her back.

"She likes you. She's usually not affectionate to everyone, but she's a pretty good judge of character."

Both Opus and Ophelia chuffed, near simultaneously.

"Did they just..."

"Yeah, you get used to it. Where can I take these critters to water the lawn?"

"Oh yeah. Sorry, just over here," he said, turning.

We followed him to a glass wall that seemed to be near the center of the hospital. It was a courtyard, surrounded by the walls of the hospital. There were benches and, in the center, a few trees with what looked like a patch of grass. It was raining cats and dogs outside, but when Doc opened the door, none of the dogs hesitated when I asked if they had to go.

Opus took off like a shot, and Sarge caught him halfway to the tree. Ophelia, as regal as ever, ran, but in a more dignified manner, making sure to look back and check on us. When they were done, they ran back to the door, shaking themselves off. Owen stirred, but I shushed him.

———

"You can put him down by me," Tina said, her voice groggy.

"He's sleeping," I told her.

"I will be too. And you need to get some sleep."

"Doc said—"

"That you can sleep in the pullout right here, with the dogs. Just... put a leash on them. We all know they don't need them, but three furballs..."

I handed her Owen, who curled against her immediately. She sat back and sighed happily.

"Are you ok?" I asked her.

I'd heard what had happened after the detectives had talked to her. She was in and out of it, but he'd given me the basics. They'd forced her at gunpoint to take the pill and go with them. Actually, the one detective had said that the gun had been pointed at my baby boy when she'd left, before it was turned and pointed in the small of her back. About twenty minutes were a total blank for her, but she remembered fighting them both off, getting the gun, and pulling the trigger. Next thing she remembered was Javier staggering at her, only to be knocked down by three furry missiles. At least, that was what the cops said she could remember. They wanted to get as much as they could in case the memory loss from the pills kicked in.

"Yeah, I'm fine. Little hazy and sleepy," she said, her hair mussed.

"I'm so glad you're ok," I told her, sitting on her side of the bed.

Opus immediately went to the built-in sofa and hopped up, claiming his spot, and the other two followed.

"Just a little bruised and probably going to have a nice shiner to go with the goose egg on the back of my head," she said, her eyes barely open. "Did the man I shot...?"

"He's alive. In surgery, but alive." I wanted to say more, but seeing her eye half swollen and knowing what had almost happened made my heart hurt.

"Good, I didn't want to do it," she said, licking her lips.

She had an IV hooked up, but I could see that her lips were cracked. I grabbed a Styrofoam cup with the straw already in it and offered it to her. She took a sip and leaned back, her eyes closing softly.

"Is it bad that I'm glad he's not dead?" she asked her eyes shut.

"It's very... you," I muttered softly.

"How bad is he?"

"You nicked something connected to his heart. From what I saw, you also got two shots into his stomach area. They are working on him."

"Did Owen see...?"

Sarge got up and came over, putting his head under her right hand, rubbing the side of his muzzle against her until she cracked an eye. She smiled, and started petting him, her motions slow and deliberate.

"I carried him on my shoulder when I let the dogs loose to find you. He might have seen you when we first got there, but I don't think he saw much of what else was going on. He was pretty upset to be in the rain and wanted you."

"I didn't want... I never would have left Owen—"

"It's ok. You didn't have any other sane choice. Besides, you were able to unleash your Kung-fu as soon as you had room and distance. You kept him safe."

"It's not Kung-fu, you nerd," she said, grinning.

Sarge started licking her arm, and I saw Tina notice; she'd quit petting him, so she started again. He groaned in pleasure.

"Your Krav Maga or however it's called. You kicked their asses. With a gun to your back, you took out two bad guys. You know there's going to be no way to keep this out of the news, don't you?"

"We can't go anywhere in public any more." Tina closed her eyes again.

"Doc says we're stuck here for a day or three."

"I already asked him... hey, it's got to be almost morning. You need sleep."

"You do too," I told her.

26

OPUS

Opus had slept off and on every chance he got since he'd had to stop the human who was trying to hurt his human Tina. He was proud that his son hadn't hesitated and had joined him in the hunt and takedown. It was similar to the training Opus had received years ago but rarely was called on to use. Today it had paid off. Ophelia had done well. She'd found the human Tina's scent before Opus did. She was leading them in her direction when Opus finally found it. He prided himself on being a good tracker, but she was light years ahead of him.

Afterwards, it was nice to get out of the rain for a while, but this big building with no carpet smelled like chemicals and sickness. The floors were cold and what limited areas to lay down and nap on were usually filled with his family. Still, he watched over them as they slept. He could nap again, but he wanted to make sure the evil squirrel ninja assassin hordes weren't in this place. Plus, he could smell something rather interesting down the hallway, which made his stomach rumble.

The food his human Rick had provided was good, but this smelled even better. Opus ignored the howling of the wind and what sounded like little rocks hitting the side of the building and focused on the smell, trying to figure out where it was.

"Knock knock," a female human voice said, before opening the door.

Rick and Tina snored, but Opus saw both Ophelia and Sarge open their eyes. This was almost a routine and it wasn't the first time he'd seen this human come and go. The others put their heads back down as the female human noted everyone sleeping. She held up a rectangular piece of plastic with paper on it and was scratching marks on the surface. Opus padded over to her, his leash dragging, and sniffed the baggy pants she wore, near her feet.

She lived near a place that had those trees that dropped the orange balls, was owned by another dog and—

She reached down and scratched behind his ears, making Opus stretch so she got the back of his neck and between the shoulders. He thought it felt amazing.

"You're a troublemaker, I can tell," she told him.

Opus sneezed at the human who laughed softly, "That's ok. You've been pretty good," she whispered, "you keep good care of these three."

Opus chuffed and saw that the pup human Owen was still snuggled in Tina's arm, the one without the plastic and metal going into it. She scratched on the board again and then walked out, leaving the door open a crack. Waiting until he could hear her move into another room, he walked over, and using his snout, pushed the door open further. No humans seemed surprised, though now it looked busier than it had earlier. Still, that smell was enticing.

The human in the white coat was at the end of the hallway, near where Opus could smell the food. He remembered how Ophelia had to carry the lazy human's bag and how amusing it was. Humans always served their dog masters faithfully, though dogs appreciated what they did. Still, the smell was tantalizing and he thought he could probably get the human to feed him again. He padded out into the hallway, dragging his leash.

The human was talking into a piece of plastic. He didn't understand how the white thing he was talking into didn't blow his ears out.

"I know, Detective," he said, "as soon as we're sure. We're following concussion protocols."

"How's the woman he attacked?" the voice from the white handle said.

"She's going to have a black eye. Might have some memory loss, but EMTs were able to confirm from your suspect that they used a roofie. We gave the antidote and pumped her full of fluids. Other than a bang to the head, those two got the worst of it."

"Did the other man make it?"

"Yes, luckily we were able to stop the bleeding quickly and work on the rest of him. He's lost a couple feet of his digestive tract, but he should make a full recovery in time."

"I'm worried the hurricane will disrupt things for us when the first one is ready to be released," the voice from the plastic handle said.

"We'll work it out, Detective... oh," he said, noticing Opus had sat down next to him and was smelling the garbage can. "What are you doing out?"

"What?" the voice said.

"Tina and Rick's Shepherd came out into the hallway."

"I heard about them. Three of them?"

"Yeah," the human doctor said, "but this is the older guy. You can tell this one has seen some things."

Opus leaned against the doctor as he started scratching between his ears. Humans were good to keep, he decided.

"I wish we had more of them on the force. Our K9 Units are going to be busy as all get out in a few hours."

Opus pulled away and stuck his nose in the trash can. He knew right where it was. He could smell it. Right there! Behind a white container!

"Stay in touch, Detective. I need to make my rounds one more time before I go to bed."

"I will. You there for the duration again like last time?"

"You know it. I'll be staying here until after the governor sounds the all clear, depending on how busy we are."

"Take care then. I'll be in touch."

The human doctor put the phone down after saying bye and noticed what Opus was doing.

"Here you go," he said, pulling the container out and opening it up.

Inside were the things his humans, Tina and Rick, liked to give Owen. Fries? What he wanted though, was on a little round half of bread.

"After surgery tonight, I couldn't eat it. Roast beef doesn't always sound good when you've put someone back together."

Opus didn't know what that meant, but two wolf-sized bites and he was devouring the meat, trying not to drool all over. When it was gone, he checked to see if there was more. Not finding any, he sat down on his rear haunch and wagged his tail, staring at the human in the white coat.

"You want more?" he asked.

Opus wagged his tail harder, his entire body wanting to shake.

"Let me see if your people are awake. I have to check on Tina anyway."

Opus stood and followed him into their room. The human Owen stirred, and Tina rolled over to face him and opened her eyes.

"Hey, buddy, you did good yesterday."

Opus wagged his tail, happy to see his human awake. He walked over and sniffed her. The chemical smell that had been coming out of her skin seemed to have gone, which made him happier. The human in the white coat did the same things the young human lady did, checking on things, talking softly to his human.

"Other than a sore spot on the back of my head, I think I'm good."

"From what we figure, you only had the Rohypnol in your system for forty-five minutes at the most. It was probably kicking in when your altercation happened."

"I think so?" she asked, her words sounding like a question to Opus.

"Hangover effects aren't uncommon with that. Actually, I'm surprised the knock to the head didn't give you one on top of everything.

"The nurse said that's why you're pumping me full of fluids," Tina said, giving him the smile Opus knew was meant to disarm the male humans.

"This is true. I need to do one last set of rounds before I head to sleep. Since none of us here are leaving during the evacuation, I'll be close by if you need me. I can take the dogs out for you if you'd like."

"That would be great. Little man will be up soon, and I didn't want to wake my husband."

"You know Opus is a certified therapy dog?" Rick asked, not opening his eyes.

"I thought you were asleep," Tina asked him.

Opus followed the conversation, his head moving side to side, then back up at the doctor.

"I will be again. Couch is sort of cold."

Ophelia decided to jump up on the couch at that point, stretching out, putting her back against Rick's.

"I didn't know that. So he's used to being in hospitals?" Doc asked.

"Last couple of years, yes. Trying to find him a quiet hobby to retire with."

Rick started snoring softly, and Opus was amused at how fast he'd fallen asleep again.

AFTER THE HUMAN HAD LET THEM RUN AND MARK territory in the only grass in the middle of this block of a building, the other two had gone back to watch over the humans. Opus had decided that none of the humans were to be out of sight of one of the pack from now on. Trouble happened when they weren't right there to watch over them. The run the night before had made him sore, but the more he moved the less it pained him.

He was following the human in the white coat who'd talked to his Tina. He'd insisted on having the leash off, so it was in a pocket of the white coat. This morning, they were visiting humans. Opus liked visiting humans early in the day. They often gave him treats and food the humans he owned rarely shared. The salty and fatty bacon that Rick loved, a sausage... real sausage not the snack that was supposed to taste like it... and all he had to do was smell them and be nice. He was good at being nice except when he walked past a room.

He stopped, his fur standing up. He knew that smell. He growled softly, becoming wrath, trembling with anticipated violence.

"Hey," the human in the white coat said, startling Opus with a hand to his collar, "you don't want to go in there. That's the guy you chewed on."

Opus stood there, staring at the door, knowing one of the people who'd hurt his pack was inside there.

"Don't worry, when this storm passes, he's getting locked up for a long time. I guess he fits some sort of profile the local PD down here has been looking for. If it's him, you did a real good job. Not everyone walked away when he went after them."

Opus's low growl changed and he went silent, looking up at the human with the white coat.

"I promise you, he's going to be stuck in there until the cops come and put him in a cage."

Opus looked between the closed door and the human and sat down, growling softly again. He knew the smell of the human. He wasn't going to budge, not until he was sure the human was locked up. The human doctor sighed and pulled the leash out of his pocket. Opus wondered if he actually thought he was going to use that to drag him away? Opus would let him put the leash on, but he wasn't going to be dragged. He'd chew his face off first.

"I'm going to put this on you, then open the door. That way you can see he's not going anywhere, ok?" the human doctor said, clipping the leash to his collar.

"Everything ok, Doctor?" a human woman in a blue baggy outfit said walking past, her eyes going from Opus to the man in the white coat.

"Yeah, fine. Sorry. This guy named Opus here understands most of what I'm saying. He's been doing my final rounds with me before I head to bed."

Opus watched the lady look at him and grin out the side of her mouth. She nodded and started walking away. He turned his attention back to the door with the man who tried to hurt his human when she heard the woman mutter "...been on shift too long."

Opus got up and pulled to the end of the leash, wanting to see the human.

"Hold on," the doc said, "don't get impatient—"

There was a loud crashing sound and the both of them turned around. Not seeing anything or seeing alerts, Doc turned back to the door he was in front of, writing the sound off as the hurricane having blown something against the wall somewhere. He pushed the latch and door open slowly then let out a gasp. Opus pushed forward, opening the door with his head and neck, pulling the human. An unconscious woman in blue clothing lay on the floor. Opus could see her chest rising and falling, but the side of her face was purple. On the side of the bed was a handcuff, one side open, the other linked around the bed rail.

"Oh shit," the doc said quietly to Opus, who'd suddenly gone still.

27

RICK

"I think we've turned our doc into a dog guy," I told Tina with an amused grin.

"I think so too. Hey, you want to get me some breakfast from the cafeteria? The whole skipping lunch and dinner thing I'm now regretting."

"You don't want to wait for when they bring you breakfast?" I asked, yawning and sitting up.

"Dayee go bye bye?" Owen asked.

"You hungry too, little man?" I asked.

"Ungee," Owen agreed, "...lisciousness"

"Deliciousness?" Tina asked me.

"I think so? I need coffee anyway. Hopefully enough to peel my eyes back awake."

"I'll be out of here soon," Tina told me, putting Owen on the ground.

He toddled over to the couch where I was, and I pulled him up. I reached for the diaper bag as he tugged at my shirt.

"What's up, buddy?" I asked him.

"Oppy?"

"Opus went with the doctor. He's got a little girl who's a patient. He called her Miss Dakota."

"Kota!" Owen told her seriously.

"Yes, Miss Dakota, so Opus is coming back here soon. After Daddy changes your britches, we'll get you some good food, ok?"

"Bar?" he asked, sticking a finger deep into his mouth.

I grinned. He had molars coming in and had been a drool monster for a bit last night. Neither Tina and I remembered when they'd started coming in, but he hadn't complained.

"You know what, how about you walk with me? We'll take the two furballs with us and see if we can get Sarge to use the bathroom again."

"Wan bar!" Owen said, sliding to the ground, looking at the door with a serious face.

"Daddy will get you one," she said over the sound of her stomach rumbling.

I picked him up and Supermanned him, making him laugh. I stopped when I saw Tina's exasperated face and put him down. She still scowled and I realized she wasn't staring at me, she was looking at the window. Somewhere, somebody had lost a potted plant. Muted by the sound of the storm and the air conditioning, the plant minus pot had blown onto the window. The rain and wind had smeared the dirt momentarily, but it was getting quickly washed away.

"Do you think we're safe up here on this floor?" Tina asked.

"Yes, but if you'd like... I can..."

"No, that's fine," Tina said.

I wasn't sure what I was going to offer to do for her. The last nurse had taken her IV out, and she was technically free to move about the room but was tired and hadn't slept well with the bed thief.

"If it gets too bad, go in the hallway, yeah?"

"I will, don't be such a worry wart!"

I gave her a little wave and walked over to pick up both leashes. Sarge ducked and ran to Tina's side of the bed where he tried to crawl up.

"You don't want to go?" she cooed to him.

"I'm not going to make him, but I figured he could take care of business before the storm gets worse."

Sarge let out a low wine and put his front paws on the bed and crawled up, laying out next to Tina. The sight made me both sad and smile at the same time. Ophelia had done much the same when it had been me in a hospital bed two years ago. Opus was lending his services elsewhere and apparently Sarge was stepping up.

"You keep your mom safe," I told him, petting him on the back.

He seemed to relax and let out a breath he'd been holding.

"Wan Bar!" Owen said, using his tiny hands to push my face to his.

"Ok, ok. Ophelia, I'm going to forget the leash, you just stick tight to me."

She let out a happy sound as I knelt and unclipped her leash.

We got to the courtyard and Ophelia refused to go out. The hurricane was pushing winds to speeds that made the square courtyard howl. When I put Owen down and cracked the door, it was almost pulled out of my hands. She just walked back and sat next to Owen. I could almost read the meaning of her body language. *If somebody is going outside, it's the dumb human.* Yeah, that would be me. The hairless monkey.

"How about we go to the cafeteria?"

"Ungry!" Owen told me, both arms lifted.

I picked him up, and Ophelia fell in as I followed my nose. Owen made faces at the nurses or people he encountered, giving a shy wave. Most would break out into a big smile and wave back, but more than a couple looked at Ophelia uneasily. A dog, off leash, at a hospital. I saw one gal seemingly have a mental battle with herself, then shrug. A hurricane was raging outside and a man walking with a dog probably wasn't even high up on the list of things she had to care about.

"There it is!"

"Down, ungry!"

I put Owen down and he took off at an almost dead run for the double glass doors. Ophelia let out a quick yip and ran ahead and in front of him, turning her body. Owen laughed and tried to go around Ophelia who changed directions, blocking and herding him.

"It's ok, girl, we'll all go then. Besides, he's getting too heavy to carry all the time. He's turning into a lump."

She let out a chuff I could barely hear as the wind and

rain intensified. Debris and other things were hitting the side of the hospital. I worried about all this glass, but it was supposedly built to withstand much worse. The radio said this was a Category 4 and unless it turned directly, we'd only be brushed by it. Still, government had evacuated the entire area as services weren't going to be available until things were safe.

I opened the door to the cafeteria, and Owen and Ophelia walked in. Owen put his hands on her collar as his legs wobbled, and she turned and licked his face. He giggled and I followed him in, rolling my eyes. There were half a dozen uniformed police officers sitting at one table with the detective I recognized from earlier. He gave me a smile and a nod as I walked up.

"Who's this fine young lady?" one of the patrolman asked.

"Ophie!" Owen told him proudly, coming to a stop next to him.

"Ophelia," I told the group.

She was pleased with the attention and wagged her tail a little less nervously than before.

"She's the one who nailed our suspect?" the detective asked.

"That was Opus and Sarge. She'll do it if asked, but with those two guys around, not usually. She's actually a trained tracker. We have done some volunteer work—"

My words cut off as one of the police officers reached over to her, two strips of bacon in his hand. She growled and he pulled his hand back, looking at me.

"Trained not to get food from strangers?" he asked me.

"I think so? She's usually a chow hound, though. Ophelia, you want some bacon?"

Her head cocked to the side and she considered my words and her tail wagged, but nervously. The patrolman handed me the bacon, and I offered it to her. She gently took one strip from my hand and dropped it to the ground where she inhaled it in a couple big bites. Owen had snatched the other piece and was attempting to force choke himself with it.

"Um, thanks," I said, watching the cop smile.

"I think she stopped me from giving the baby the bacon," the patrolman said to me.

I thought about that and it made sense. Ophelia had never seen us allowing a stranger to give food to the baby. With her training she probably was buying me time to make up my mind. When I'd made a decision, she'd gone along with it. I was starting to think my dogs were smarter than me.

"That makes sense. What are you guys doing?" I asked.

"Only place in town open for breakfast," one said around a mouthful of biscuits and gravy.

My stomach grumbled.

"Plus the hospital is on high ground. We can park our patrol cars here and dispatch can radio in what's needed. Better than sitting in the car in the middle of this," another one said, motioning outside where the storm had turned the sky into a roiling black mass.

"True. And... the scenery isn't half bad," Detective Hanson said.

I followed his gaze to a table where younger twenty

something nurses were all chatting. A couple noticed our attention and they turned back to their table; laughter rang out and the one who'd caught the detective staring had a creeping redness on her neck and ears.

"I think she's caught you looking before," another patrolman ribbed him.

"I hate talking to women," he said suddenly, "I never know how to break the ice."

I knelt down. "Owen, you see that pretty nurse in the blue and white?" I said, pointing.

"Momma pretty?" he asked me, a finger going to his mouth to pick at the remnants of the bacon.

"Yes, she's pretty like mommy. Go say hi."

"Oh tay," Owen said with a smile and started for the group.

"What are you doing?" Hanson asked.

"Matchmaking."

The guys were laughing, but not as loud and raucously as the ladies had, because they saw Owen was actually going through with it. Both tables full of people watched as my tiny human went to the gal who vaguely looked like Tina. She even had similar glasses, but was a little less gazelle and more gentle curves.

"What's that?" she asked as he pulled on her sleeve.

"Dayee, more, po!" Owen said loud enough for us to hear. "Pull," he said, taking a finger in both hands and pulling on her.

"Ok, ok," she said, looking over.

Ophelia sat on her hind end, her tail going a mile a minute and her tongue hanging out.

"Did you ever doubt me?" I asked her, dropping a hand to her head to give her a pet.

Ophelia barked excitedly as the nurse followed Owen back to me.

"I'm not quite sure what he was asking, but sounded like he said daddy?" she asked me.

"Actually, he was asking you to come over here. I asked him to introduce you to Detective Hanson here," I said, nodding to the plain clothes detective.

He shot me a panicked look, but her smile lit her face and this time he was the one who was turning red in the face. Ophelia hesitated before finally getting up and running over to her. She pushed with her muzzle making the nurse turn to see why she was getting pushed.

"What's she doing?" she asked me as Ophelia herded her around the table.

"I know what she's doing," one of the patrolmen said, getting up and offering her his seat. "I'm going to head upstairs and check on the prisoner anyway. See you guys."

The nurse sat down in the vacated seat next to Hanson, and everybody at two tables was watching the two of them, the other people having gone silent figuring out something was going on.

"Hi," Detective Hanson said, then shot me a look of pure evil.

"Hi there, Detective. Nice to see you again."

"Again?" one of the others asked in a falsetto voice.

"He comes in here for breakfast three days a week and then goes to the Pediatric Chemo Clinic and reads to the kids, or plays video games with him."

He looked at his plate, where he was rearranging eggs and hash browns, then up at us, almost daring us to say something.

"It's nice seeing you again, Cindy," he said, breaking into a smile. "I noticed you on the pediatric floor more and more lately?"

"I love working with the kids," she said. "Someday... I would never wish cancer on any kid, but someday if I have kids, I want them to be as brave as the kids I help take care of."

"Ungry!" Owen said, pulling on my finger.

I'd been watching the unfolding drama and romance, and although I'd kept track of the baby man, I had forgotten what we had come for.

"Let's get some food," I told him. "Ladies and gentlemen, nice to see you again!" I backed up slowly as Ophelia gave them a high pitched yip before turning to follow me.

Owen fell in place and when we got near the serving area I had to push him back gently, telling him it was hot. He repeated the word as I filled three plates with eggs, ham, bacon, biscuits and gravy on another, with sausage links. Then a plate of just meat, more bacon, sausage and ham. Owen was asking for a bar and french fries, the only two foods he never refused, but I was snagging silverware as the cashier rang me up at the end of the food line.

"Don't get too far from me," I told Owen as Ophelia made the same conclusion I did.

He laughed as she walked in front of him, herding him back my way, giving him a lick.

"She's so good with him," the cashier said.

"People don't own dogs, dogs own people. She's sort of adopted him. Ophelia had a litter of pups the same time he was born."

"My daughter has a boxer that's like that. Protective dogs," she told me, handing my change back.

"They're great at that," I agreed and saw three patrolmen get up and head out the door in a hurry, probably having gotten a call.

"Let's go sit down," I told Owen, noting the now empty chairs near Detective Hanson and Nurse Cindy.

"Wan Juice!"

"You want juice?" I asked to make sure because the wind had picked up and the last couple cops' radios started crackling.

"Juice cuppy!" Owen said, pulling on the leg of my shorts.

I was glad I'd brought the little backpack that held an extra cup and bottle. I was even more surprised by how little pushback I was getting having the dogs in here.

"Do you get a lot of service dogs in here?" I asked the cashier suddenly.

"Quite a few. I don't think I've seen your girl here before."

"Grammy wuv Oppy, Oofie, and Barge!" Owen said loudly. "Owie wan juice now?"

"Ok," I said laughing, "he's telling you his grandma loves his Opus, Ophelia, and Sarge also."

"Those all your dogs?" she asked as Owen pulled at my finger.

"Yeah, the other two are upstairs with my wife and Doc."

"I hope you folks plan on sticking around until this wind lets up. It might not be safe outside for three fur babies and this rascal."

I knew what she meant, the hurricane winds were blowing debris into the courtyard, we could see it through one of the glass walls of the café. Debris from outside the center portion of the hospital. Despite the glass, I felt safer inside than the outside.

"We're planning on sticking around until it's safe to leave," I told her.

"You three stay out of shenanigans," she said, a matronly smile crossing her face.

We took our trays to the table where Detective Hanson was sitting with Cindy. His face looked concerned and pinched. He motioned for me to sit. I put the trays down and pulled a seat out for Owen. He climbed up in it awkwardly.

"I'll be right back, I need to grab some coffee," I told them.

"Javier got out of his cuffs and assaulted a nurse," Hanson blurted.

I sat down instead of heading for coffee.

TINA & SARGE

s soon as Rick and Owen left with Ophelia, Tina kicked Sarge off the bed and stretched out. It felt glorious to have an entire bed to herself. Sarge sat next to her, then laid down on the floor as she got comfortable. She pulled one of the blankets up and, ignoring her rumbling stomach, she rolled on her side. She was still sleepy, either a result of the knock on the head, the drug, or just plain exhaustion. Still, the wind howled and things made banging and crashing sounds outside the room.

SARGE DRIFTED ALSO. IN HIS DREAMS, HE WAS FOLLOWING his alpha into another fight. The man who'd tried to hurt his human had already shown his stomach and was retreating, holding a bloody arm, when the smell hit him. The bad man was going away, yet he could smell him getting closer. His leg twitched as the door seemingly opened, snapping the dog awake. Sarge growled low and then heard a loud bark further away, his alpha, his father. The human Tina also woke up with a start, but Sarge was moving to the door.

Every guard hair on his body stood up, and the ridge along his back did as well. Something more than the dream made him instinctively want to fight. To protect. To make his enemies quake in fear for even daring to hurt the humans he was entrusted to care for. Another bark, then the slapping of feet. Sarge used his nose to push the door open to see Opus flash past the room. More slapping of the feet and the man in the white coat was running after the leash that had been dropped. Or, more than likely, that Opus had pulled out of his grip.

Sarge wanted to follow, but his duty lay with this tiny human woman. His father was on the case, and he'd learned everything he could from his father. Protect the humans first, fight and conquer the enemies second.

"What is it, boy?" Tina said, "Did I hear Opus?"

Sarge cocked his head to the side, considering her question, then turned and jumped on her bed from almost five feet away. She sat back in shock, pushing at his body, but he put his nose down and pushed back at her hands, then turned and laid down on her legs.

"Get off me, you big doofus," Tina complained.

Sarge just looked at her with big brown eyes. His human wasn't going anywhere, and neither was he.

29

OPUS

Opus let out a bark as soon as he caught the scent of the bad human. He'd pulled against the leash so hard that the man in the white coat was forced to let it go. Then he'd taken off, giving a hunting bark, both to let the prey know the game was on, and to alert Ophelia and Sarge. They both had jobs to do protecting humans, but the bad man might try to go in their direction. Better they were forewarned.

Opus shot between the legs and a walker of an elderly patient who let out a surprised laugh as he made his way toward the bottom of the building. Opus knew about the metal boxes that took you up and down, but not how to use them. He skid to a stop next to a door, thinking hard. He could smell the outside stronger here. He pushed the door with his muzzle, but it didn't budge. He took half a step back trying to figure out what to do while listening to the human in the white coat chase after him.

There was a silver flashy handle. Opus pushed

himself to his hind legs and looked out the square glass above the handle, his paws resting against the door. It was slick and his front paws slipped, but not before he saw stairs. Those he understood. Some went toward the clouds, some went toward the smell of the ocean. As he was sliding down to all fours, his paw brushed the handle and the door pushed forward. The opening almost had him falling in an undignified manner, so he hurried. The door swung half shut when he was halfway in, but his body prevented the door from closing. He pushed past until he heard a click.

Smelling the bad man's smell heading in the direction of down and the ocean, Opus went for the stairs, only to be pulled up short. The red leash the Doc had used was wedged in the bottom of the door. Opus let out a frustrated bark that echoed on the tiled surfaces of the stairwell, making his ears hurt. The slapping of feet outside seemed to stop and then the door opened. As soon as Opus felt the leash free, he hurried down the stairs as fast as his legs would take him, being mindful of not tripping on the dragging leash.

"Opus," the human in the white coat yelled.

Every part of his body wanted to stop, but Opus decided to ignore the command; he didn't own this human, and he had to make sure the bad man was nowhere near any of his people. He continued down, determined to hunt down the man who'd almost hurt his woman. He knew Sarge was taking care of his Tina, and Ophelia would die in her efforts to protect Owen and his human Rick. No, the man running away was Opus's, and this time he wouldn't be going for the arm if the bad man tried to hurt his humans.

His rear leg ached and his hearing was distracted by the sounds of the storm raging outside, but he could hear the Doc yelling his name before following. Opus let out another bellowing bark and kept pushing through.

30

OWEN & RICK

Bacon is good. Owen knew bacon was good, because it went yummy in his tummy. He tried to listen as the guy in the suit told his dad what was going on. He didn't understand much of it, and how his dad was becoming increasingly nervous and agitated. Owen didn't know these words, but he understood the feelings. He offered his dad a sausage, only to have it put back on the plate. Talk, talk, talk. All big people did was talk. Owen took a bite of the sausage and decided to change tactics.

"This?" Owen asked, a handful of bacon.

"Not right now, buddy," Rick told him.

Owen wanted to pout, but bacon was so good. Ophelia wagged her tail, and Owen gave her the piece he'd tried to give his dad. She took it, wolfing it down, then came back for more. Owen was going to get another piece, but she was licking his hand, then his face. It tickled, and he laughed. A distant bark had both Owen and Ophelia look in that direction. He wasn't sure that was what he'd heard because of all the big booming and crashing outside. He grabbed more sausage and bacon and slid off his seat. Ophelia looked at him nervously, but Owen offered her more bacon.

While she was tracking that, a man ran past the cafeteria. Owen followed the movement, not making out the features very well. That was when he heard another bark.

"Oppy!" he told Ophelia who was cleaning his hand again while he was stuffing a bite of sausage in his mouth with the other.

Ophelia whined to Owen and when he tried to move toward the bark, she got in front of him and pushed him back with her body. Thunder crashed suddenly and the hospital went dark. Owen moved forward, knowing he'd heard his Oppy, and wanting to give him the rest of his bacon. The dark didn't bother Owen, he was fine with it, unlike his parents. He knew the direction he'd seen the man go in and heard the bark from, so he walked that way as the lights went dark. He stopped a moment, then kept going, not afraid of the dark.

The cafeteria's glass doors had been wedged open earlier by a cleaner, and Owen walked right out of them while people worried about why the emergency lights weren't kicking right back on. Owen heard another bark in front of him and toddled in that direction. He heard something bang, then a gust of wind almost knocked him down. The glass wall, it moved and was pushing him back. Owen put both hands on the glass and pushed with as much strength as his little arms and legs could. He wanted his Oppy to have the bacon.

I KNEW OWEN WAS BORED, AND I FELT BAD IGNORING HIM while I talked with the detective. He was telling me to stay calm and that the first patrolman who'd gone upstairs was already outside of Tina's room. She was safe there. The hospital had been put on lock down, and there was no way to exit the hospital. Suddenly, the lights went out and thunder crashed and Ophelia barked somewhere past me, probably chasing after something Owen dropped or threw.

"Shit," the detective said in the darkness.

Lightning flashed outside, illuminating things for a brief second. I felt for Owen and found that the seat next to me was empty.

"Ophelia?" I called loudly as lightning flashed again.

I felt her brush against my leg, her body trembling, but she was pulling at me. She emitted a low whining sound, a sense of urgency. Lightning flashed again and I saw Owen's seat was empty.

"Owen?" I called, standing up.

"Is he under the table?"

"No," I said, using my phone's flashlight app, having to fight Ophelia's urgent tugging. "Where is he?" I asked, suddenly realizing that she was trying to pull me to go find the baby.

She let go and spun in a circle, whining.

"What's she doing?" the detective asked.

I ignored him. "Can you find Owen?" I asked Ophelia as lightning flashed, lighting up the cafeteria.

The emergency lights kicked on at that moment,

washing the room in a soft glow. They weren't as bright as the normal lights were, but I could see that the cafeteria was empty other than us. I also saw the doors we'd come in had been wedged open sometime afterward. I felt a lump in my throat and a chill ran down me, making my arms break out in gooseflesh. I wanted to scream, I wanted to cry. Ophelia barked loudly and I focused on her. I pulled the leash out and she sat down. I think she instinctively knew she didn't need the leash as much as I did. She was already two steps ahead of me.

"What are you doing?"

"My dog is going to lead me to Owen," I told him, once more looking around the cafeteria to make sure there wasn't anywhere he could have hidden or gotten lost.

If he was still in this room, Ophelia would have herded him immediately back to me. Her behavior scared me because it showed that, somehow, he'd given everyone the slip. Still, she was a tracker of exceptional talent, and the leash was for me to be able to keep following her if the lights went out again. She probably didn't even need her eyesight to follow Owen, and he'd only been gone maybe fifteen or twenty seconds before we'd noticed. He couldn't have gone far. I clipped on the leash.

"Take me to my son," I told her.

I wasn't pulled so much as dragged. Ophelia was the quieter and gentler of the three dogs, more of a lover than a fighter. Opus, in all his goofy glory, had no problem flipping the switch from family dog to a terribly aggressive furry missile, while Sarge was still finding his groove, but definitely more on the aggressive side than either of his parents. That was why it surprised me when she nearly pulled me off my feet, choking herself.

The lights blinked again and went out. I nearly ran into Ophelia who'd stopped as well, but I was hit from behind. I'd forgotten about Detective Hanson. I hit the ground hard, losing the leash. We tried to untangle ourselves and, as I was pushing myself to my hands and knees, the lights flickered again. Ophelia was on the far side of the hallway, near the courtyard, barking loudly from our side of the glass doors before going silent.

"Sorry, I did a double check of the cafeteria and then started running this way as soon as—"

"She isn't the one barking," I said quietly, scrambling to my feet as I had already started running, hearing the deeper booming bark.

I heard Hanson behind me, but was focused on the door. Twenty fast steps. I heard snarling now, and somebody screaming on the other side of the glass, despite the raging wind and rain that had all but drowned out all other sound. I almost went through the glass when I didn't stop my momentum in time. Ophelia was off like a shot as soon as I hit the door latch, spilling us both into a torrential downpour. I could barely see. The wind was blowing water and all sorts of things into my eyes, and I was immediately soaked. Instead, I took half a breath and listened, ignoring my stinging eyes.

I heard Ophelia let out a hunting bark, then a louder, deeper growl straight ahead of me. I put an arm over my eyes and lowered myself and pushed against the wind. The lights inside suddenly got brighter, all around the hospital, as the main power came back on, and some-where behind me I heard the door slam shut, with Hanson's cursing alerting me I had backup.

"...No! I won't let you!!" I heard an accented voice screaming.

"Ophelia?" I called.

She hadn't been the barking I'd originally heard. Was there another dog in this part of the hospital? Then it hit me; I recognized the tone of the growling and snarls. Ophelia gave a loud, high-pitched bark. I kept pushing on in their direction until I could make out two furry forms, both rigid and, despite being soaked, their fur standing straight up.

"...Just let me get the kid inside," somebody pleaded, but they weren't talking to me.

Opus must have heard me, because he looked back in my direction and then straight ahead. I wiped my eyes and got in line with the dogs. The man who had attacked my wife was standing there, his clothing plastered to his body, holding Owen against his chest, one arm shielding his head.

"Give me my son," I said, my growl on par with Opus's.

"Those dogs, man... the boy followed us out and I scooped him up; the damn dog won't let me get him back inside. I'll put him down as soon as—"

"Give me my son," I told him. "Sit," I said in English and noted that both came to rigid attention as I walked forward.

"They won't attack me?" he asked, then he must have recognized me.

"No, unlike what you were going to do to my wife," I said, my voice going low.

"I just want out of here man," he said, holding Owen out.

"You!" Hanson said as I took Owen.

He babbled something, wiping his eyes. His blond hair was plastered to his face and somehow he'd gotten smudged with enough dirt that the downpour hadn't washed a streak off his face.

"I'm sorry, I panicked and—"

"You're under arrest again, you have the right—"

"Hold on, Detective," I said, holding Owen tight, then turned.

"Mr. Rick?" he asked, confused as I gently pushed Owen into his arms.

I turned and sucker punched Javier in the gut as hard as I could. He instinctively doubled over as the wind left him. It was convenient because my other fist was coming up from below my own belt. The uppercut hit him off center, but it was enough to knock him off his feet. I heard Hanson curse. I turned, shaking my aching hand, as he handed Owen back to me and pulled out the cuffs. Both Opus and Ophelia whined from about five feet behind me. I turned, cradling Owen's head to my shoulder.

"You did great," I told them both.

Opus' chuff was audible over the sounds of the storm. Ophelia's tail was wagging in the water and filth that the hurricane was throwing, but she was visibly happy.

"Come here, you goofballs," I told them.

"My Oppy and Ooofie," Owen said, surprisingly

upbeat and nonchalant about it all, despite the way the storm seemed to push rain in all directions.

"Yes, your Opus and Ophelia," I told him.

"Bacon?" he asked, dropping a handful of smashed meat that the wind carried away.

Opus watched as the greasy crumbles were lost in the semi darkness with something like longing, but when I looked up again I saw he had his tongue hanging out.

"You did it again, buddy," I told him, hearing retching behind me.

I reached a hand out to pet Opus and Ophelia who were suddenly all about getting pet. My hand was sore and I could see it swelling already. I ignored the commotion behind me, but a second later Hanson and Javier fell into step with me and the dogs as I walked in the direction I thought the door was in to get back inside the building.

"ONLY YOU," TINA SAID FROM THE DRIVER'S SEAT.

"What'd I do?" I asked her, my feet kicked up on the dash, my laptop open.

"Now I know why you're an introvert," Tina said.

I avoided commenting that she looked like she needed a phonebook or two to sit on. Our size difference wasn't something I usually noticed any more, except she was driving my big van and we were a day out from Michigan still.

"Why's that?" I asked her.

"Whenever we go on somewhere, things seem to

happen. It's like… if you wrote this kind of stuff in your books, nobody would believe it really happened."

"Sometimes life is stranger than fiction," I told her, "Something about suspension of disbelief."

"Leaf!" Owen shouted from behind me.

I turned and held up my casted right hand. He pushed his against it, our own version of knuckles.

"I mean, those guys attacked me but I was ok. Last year in Utah—"

"We don't have to talk about this," I told her.

"You don't want to?" she asked.

"No, I mean, if you don't want to talk about the bad stuff specifically. I know your dreams still get to you is all."

"Listen, babe," Tina said, "I will never be a victim again. Even when those guys drugged me, I had things under control. You and the dogs coming when you did probably saved Javier's life. So I… I think I proved that I can take care of myself. After being afraid for all this time, I really think the dreams won't be an issue."

"But last night—"

"I dreamed about how fearless our two-year-old terrorist is and how nothing seems to bug him. I thank Jesus everyday that he brought me you and the dogs. If he had a little more fear in him, I wouldn't worry so much, but I have you and the dogs."

"Yeah," I said, wondering where this was going.

"It just really bugs me though."

"What does?" I asked her, thinking this was a change of subject.

"When you found Javier, he thought he was

protecting Owen from the dogs. He could have finished crossing the courtyard and gone out the emergency exit, but he stopped for some reason and shielded him from the storm and the dogs."

"Ok?"

"What I'm saying is... you still sucker punched him," she said, turning to look at me.

My left hand was casted almost from elbow to fingertips and had caused us to wait another half a day after the storm had finished blowing through. We'd been able to get out as soon as it did and the extra fuel we'd stored had been a good call, because much of Florida and Georgia were dry from the evacuations.

"Yeah, that felt good," I admitted.

"But he was trying to save our son."

"No, when Opus caught up with him, he was sort of using him as a shield. Maybe even a bargaining chip to escape. He wasn't trying to help or save you earlier either. Wasn't he the guy who knocked me over after I'd been drugged?"

"I guess the reason I'm mad at you..." Her words trailed off and she grinned as my jaw dropped open, "I'm just kidding, I'm not mad. I just... this is so surreal."

"Almost like we're stuck in somebody else's story?" I asked her.

"Exactly. But I hope you can use this in your writing somehow. Beating those guys asses helped me mentally get over some things. I hope you can write this mess out of your system, or however you choose to deal with this."

"You know what I really want to do?" I asked her suddenly.

"Grammy?!" Owen shouted.

"Exactly," I told Owen, turning to see a grin so cheesy it was straight outta Wisconsin.

"You want to go up north?"

"Or see if Annette wants to come down and stay with us for a few days. You know how often she's called us once she could."

"I like that idea." Tina said, "Either way, but... I might need to heal up some. Your van is a pain to drive."

Opus chuffed from the spot in the middle of us, rubbing his head first on Tina, then taking a step to me and laying his big head across the keys of my laptop. I scratched his head with my right hand, making him groan in pleasure.

"So no more super adventures?" Tina asked.

"I'm all for adventure, let's just take the danger out of it."

"Wuv Mommy n Dayee!" Owen yelled for the eleventy billionth time.

"Love you too, bud," I said at the same time as Tina.

We both looked at each other and chorused, "Jinx,"

Tina silently laughed, and I sat there quietly until Ophelia pushed next to Opus and sniffed my cast. Her whiskers tickled my fingers.

"Dang it, Rick, I release you from your Jinx. You can't type and, if you can't talk, stories don't get written."

"Ok, but you owe me a coke," I told her.

"In the cooler, sugar," she said watching I-75.

"Ok, if you don't care, I think I'm going to get my recorder out and work on a story here in a little bit. It's kind of burning the forefront of my head."

"What's it about?" Tina asked.

"Not my usual stuff. It's about a moonshiner in Arkansas."

"What's romantic and sexy about that?" Tina asked me.

"No, it's not a romance. It's a post-apocalyptic book."

"Oooh! So you are going to finally finish that storyline you started on earlier this week?"

"Yes, ma'am," I said, feeling a little self-conscious.

"I read your notes and outline for it. There's only one thing missing in the story."

"What's that?" I asked her.

"Your main character, Wes... he needs a dog."

Opus loudly barked in agreement while Ophelia gave me a high-pitched whine.

"Oggy!" Owen said loudly over the sound of the wind and a window that was opened a crack.

"Yes, a doggy," I told him, "Every boy and girl should have one."

My words weren't just for him. They were for me, for Tina, and anybody who'd listen. A dog gives the purest form of love a human can get, with the exception of their kids or their spouse. Dogs have an overwhelming love coupled with honor, dignity, and a purity that we humans lack. Maybe, just maybe, I was reminding myself.

--The End--

To be notified of new releases, please sign up for my mailing list at: **http://eepurl.com/bghQbI**

AUTHOR'S NOTE

This was the hardest book of the Opus series to write. It's been almost a year and a half since I lost Beastly and I'm still missing him. I have a son whose nickname is 'Hemmy' or the 'The Little Tyrant', here in the house. As I grew, as my son grew, the story here seemed to grow as well.

I put an Easter egg at the end of this book, leading into another series I have about an EOTWAWKI situation, where the main character also has a canine companion.

As always, thank you for reading the story! Feel free to contact me via Facebook or email at boyd3@live.com

ABOUT THE AUTHOR

Boyd Craven III was born and raised in Michigan, an avid outdoorsman who's always loved to read and write from a young age. When he isn't working outside on the farm, or chasing a household of kids, he's sitting in his Lazy Boy, typing away.

You can find the rest of Boyd's books on Amazon & Select Book Stores.

boydcraven.com
boyd3@live.com

Made in the USA
Lexington, KY
20 August 2019